Praise for Nel Stephenson
and *The Day of Forgetting*

"A wild page-turner that packs big-ticket secrets till the very end."

-Elyn Saks, author, The Center Cannot Hold (Hachette)

~

"A riveting thriller with twists and turns on every page until the electrifying, brilliantly plotted end."

-Skye Moody, author of eleven novels (St. Martins)

~

"Mischievous and philosophical."

-Nikita Lalwani, author of three novels (Viking)

THE **DAY** OF **FORGETTING**

A PANDEMIC THRILLER

NEL STEPHENSON

Lightspeed
Books

Published by Lightspeed Books. Lightspeed Books and its logo are trademarks of Lightspeed Books, inc.

Library of Congress Cataloging-in-Publication Data available.

Pbk ISBN: 978-1-952087-03-5

Audio ISBN: 978-1-952087-04-2

Ebook ISBN: 978-1-952087-05-9

Cover design by Dane Low

Manufactured in the United States of America

*Here's to writers' tears—and their dazzling words
that help us bear the tedium of life.*

1

Chen

I'm standing in front of a rookie bank teller who hasn't figured out how to make a decent knot in his tie. I have no idea why my mind went blank. I don't even know who the devil I am. But I see instantly that I'm at the temple of the Almighty Dollar. Not a bad place to be. I'm squeezing something in my sweaty hand. I look down to see what it is. Some wrinkled piece of paper, with this scribbled on it: "Give me 50K or I'll shoot you all."

Holy shit. That's no good. I look at the teller boy to figure out what's going on, but he's a bag of nerves. I pat my pockets. No gun. Nope, didn't drop it either. All around me, customers and bank people are standing around or sitting on sofas, acting all dreamy and spaced out. But no one is hiding under the desk or dropping to the floor. When in doubt, act cool, man.

I spot five sealed wads of cash and a plastic grocery bag, all sitting on the counter. That's when I realize a transaction is already in progress. Maybe he was about to give me the goods without freaking everybody out. I crumple the damning scrap of paper, and jam it into my boxer shorts.

"Dude, I'm in a hurry," I tell the fellow, pointing to the pile, like it's coming out of my own goddamn bank account. "I'd like my money now."

The wiry teller looks at me blankly, then pushes the stacks of cash towards me before I know what to do with them.

"The bag too," I say, hoping that doesn't stretch my luck.

I walk out of there real slow, trying to look casual, going about my own business. Underneath all that, I'm feeling nervous and funny, and my brain is still AWOL. In the parking lot, folks look like they've just landed on a new planet. They're staring at car keys in their hands, gawking at their faces in visor mirrors. Everybody's dazed and confused. I am too, come to think of it. If I really just robbed a bank, why the hell am I blanking on my escape plan?

That's when four LAPD cruisers pull right into the parking lot, their lights flashing, in stealth mode. Shit. Before I can disappear somewhere, the cops pop out of their vehicles. I'm feeling real faint. I glance back, but the cops don't make five steps before a bunch of people badger them with questions.

Hey, maybe they didn't come for me, after all. I stamp out the jitters and keep walking, as slowly as I can, till I turn the corner. I duck into a Starbucks and plan to head straight for the john, where I can hide, secure my cash, and figure out what the fuck is going on with me. Inside the coffee shop, folks are huddled around a laptop with the volume on high. It's only when I hear the news blaring out about some weird mass amnesia that I understand what a lucky son of a bitch I am. The memory wipe-out hit right smack in the middle of a bank robbery gone wrong. The bank teller must've pressed the panic button somewhere in between pulling out the cash and forgetting what just happened. That's why the L.A. police just arrived on the scene. My ass could've been hauled to jail.

I sit myself on the toilet lid, take a deep breath, then pull my money out. It's calming to count green. Right under the plastic sheathing, there's a one-hundred-dollar bill on either side. In between the wads, though, turns out they're all ten-dollar bills. Shameless cheapskates. That's a far cry from fifty grand. Still, I try to look at things in the positive. I got something out of nothing. And I'm still out on the street.

I hang in the john for a while, waiting till the police go on to bigger messes. There are old car keys in my pocket—but I have no idea which one is my vehicle out there. Might have to wait till everybody's cleared out. There's no address in my wallet, no keys for any digs anywhere. My driver's license is from Massachusetts—like I'm gonna drive across the country to go back to a place that isn't even worth remembering. Waste of gas. Better weather in California, anyways. Still, this fog in my brain doesn't feel too good. It's kinda creepy not knowing who I am, if I've got brothers somewhere.

When I poke out of the Starbucks after dark, the cops are gone. A few people are crying on street corners. An old lady harasses me for money to take a cab back home. Who the hell begs for cab fare? I mean, if you're broke, take a bus, lady. I'm not feeling real generous, especially as the granny's wearing fancy sunglasses as big as coasters. But she can smell cash on me and won't let go. I'm fishing in my pocket for a fiver, but I pull out a twenty instead. She grabs the bill out of my hand, tells me God bless, and takes off. Jeez.

Only two vehicles are left in the parking lot: a blue Beemer and a rusty old red Hyundai next to it. My keys are old so I try the Hyundai, but the jumpy Beemer alarm goes off anyway. As I get in the beater, I hear the half-hearted hiccup of police sirens—the noise they make when they don't know what to do next.

If I try to skedaddle, they'll assume I tried to steal the Beemer. So I slump all the way down, and struggle to offload the five wads in the dark, greasy space underneath the seats. I stow four of them before the cops park their vehicle so close that there's no telling if the cruiser camera is right on me. I've got no choice but to stick the last wad in my baggy pants. Two officers get out and head for the wailing Beemer. They're talking loud over the alarm, like they own the place.

Oh, no. I slide down my seat some more, hoping they don't see me. These two are so close, it gives me goose bumps. I pretend to sleep, my head buried in my hoodie, when I hear a knock on my window.

"Hey, look who's in here," says one of them.

I don't move.

"Get out of the car. Put your hands behind your head," says the officer, his nervous hand on his holster.

2

Max

Before I even open my eyes, I know something is wrong. The world is too silent, as if all the voices have been switched off. I'm hiding behind a collapsed wall for a reason I don't remember. Behind me is a pile of rubble; above me, a violent sun. Shielding my eyes, I look through a gap in the bricks. In the distance there's a hovel, whitewashed in another century, and a gutted building. I almost look right past the man hiding behind a post, if it weren't for his entire shadow spilled on the white earth like a puddle. Only his military boot is sticking out—and his Kalashnikov.

A rush of adrenaline floods me with fear. Not only am I not armed, but my brain is not working right. I have no memory of how I got here, where I am, who I am.

Right at my feet, is a video camera that landed lens first in the dirt. It's plastered with a yellow sticker that reads 'Property of The New York Times.' The recording light is still on. I lean over to pick it up. That's when I see a badge poking out of my pocket. PRESS is printed on it in screaming letters, and France/U.S. It may as well say 'shoot me.' I must be a Western journalist on the frontlines, somewhere desiccated, like Africa or the Middle East. Why don't I have a fixer with me, or at least a bulletproof vest? I must be incredibly brave or actively suicidal.

I zoom in on the armed man, trying to understand the situation. Just like that, he leaves his cover, his military issue uniform now in full view. He jogs towards a figure on the ground: a teenage boy, a spill of blood disgorging from his blue jeans. I want to help the kid, but I'm frozen behind the camera, intimidated by the machine gun. So much for incredibly brave. The soldier uses his scarf to tie a tourniquet around the boy's thigh. The kid doesn't move, because he's already gone. What a shitty job I have, filming people dying. The soldier spits on the ground, and walks away from the corpse, his black shadow stalking him. I'm glad to see him go, and start breathing again.

"Hands up," says a voice behind me.

Shit. It's another fellow with the same uniform, aiming a pistol at my head. This one's taller, wears a sling on his left arm, and speaks broken English.

"Get out," he says, and whistles to his buddy.

I have no choice but to climb out of my hideout. The tourniquet guy runs over, grabs my video camera and backpack, and pats me down. The whole time, he's screaming in my face in a foreign language. He's breaking my balls so much I want to slap him. But there's nothing like a gun to remind you of your manners.

"Where from?" asks the taller one.

"France," I say, hearing my French accent for the first time. I'm disoriented, but I know better than to reveal my US connection without knowing what country or cause they're fighting for.

"Let's go," he says, still aiming the weapon at me.

We pass by four bodies on the ground, their blood mostly dry. I force myself to look at the boy's face. It feels like my job to be his last witness. His eyes are already staring into another world—hopefully a better one.

They lead me to the nearby hovel, where they've been camping out. The soldier with the sling frowns as he inspects his pistol for bullets. Supplies must be meager.

"Sit," he says, pointing to the concrete floor. "What you film?"

"I don't know," I say.

"Play. See it." He brings a stubby index finger to his eye. Who knows on how many people this one finger has pulled the trigger.

I'm not sure I can work the camera. My brain is missing in action, but it's best to keep that to myself. With sweaty, trembling fingers, I somehow coax the machine to replay the clip. Both soldiers hover above me, their eyes on the small screen.

The footage starts with graffiti on the gutted building: 'Death to Assad, Victory to Syria.' I'm definitely suicidal to have come here. I don't understand why I remember the Syrian civil war, but not my own name. My memory is patchy. These two must be in Assad's army. Looks like I filmed a long exchange of gunfire. I put the recording on fast forward: the skirmish ends with my two captors shooting the three rebels dead, whose bodies we saw on the way here. On camera, the teenager in jeans is still alive—and darts out of the ruins to throw a stone. He misses, but the tourniquet guy shoots him anyway. It sickens me that all I could do for the kid was quietly film his death. What dirty work. Half witness, half vulture.

Then the camera view drops to the floor, like I decided to film my boots. For a second during the fall, the camera captures what must be my own face. Skinny; pale; with the eyes of a caged cheetah. Is that really me?

The last thing I'd filmed was what just happened: the soldier abandoning his cover to put a tourniquet on the same kid he'd shot moments before. That's not normal. His brain is not working right either.

The one with the sling turns to me and points to his head.

"You have problems?"

I nod. So they must have something going on too.

"Bomb?" he asks.

The camera recorded no blasts, no dust clouds, no ground shaking.

"No bomb," I say.

"Chemical?" he asks in a suspicious tone.

I shrug, but something tells me none of Assad's chemical weapons are this kind to living things.

One of them flicks on an old portable TV sitting over a crate. The Al Jazeera broadcaster looks shell-shocked, her hair in disarray. I don't understand a word and there are no English captions. A shaky, amateur video shows masses of people swarming out of skyscrapers in Manhattan, panic-stricken.

I immediately think another terrorist attack. But then they also show footage from London and Tokyo, where people are abandoning their cars, sitting on sidewalks, confused.

My captors are suddenly huddled over the television set, mesmerized by the news. It's my one chance to inch over to the video camera, and pretend to replay the clip. I figure out a way to remove the memory card, and discreetly slip it in my sock. The taller guy glares at me.

"Don't move," he says, stroking his weapon.

What's wrong with me, risking my life for a memory

card? Luckily, he hasn't seen me doing anything, engrossed as he is in the videos of aimless crowds that keep cycling on TV. This time, they include English captions about a global state of emergency, a collective amnesia. Amnesia? That's what I have, some kind of partial amnesia. That's what these two must have also.

In reaction to the news, the soldiers start babbling like a pot of boiling water. The tourniquet guy tries to use his cell phone, but it's dead. He grabs my backpack and dumps the contents on the floor. It looks like a secondhand bazaar: cigarettes, an empty water bottle, stale bread, a wallet, a cell phone, airline tickets, an EU passport, and a medical kit with a sterile syringe. I want to reach for my wallet, my passport. But the bastard pockets both, as well as my cigarettes, and starts making a call with my cell. While he's shouting on the phone, his back to me, the taller one hovers over the TV trying to dial up the volume.

This could be my only chance to get the hell out of here while they're confused. If only I could read my name off the plane tickets. But it's better to have a life than a name.

I bolt out of the shack and run for it, hoping they won't waste a bullet killing me.

3

Max

Only when I round the corner of the gutted building do I look back. No one's chasing me. They've gotten everything there is to get from me, the bastards. On the street, men wander around, adrift, staring at each other. One man's shirt is sprayed with dried blood, but he doesn't even seem to notice. I slow down and try to blend in, as though I'm not the only Westerner. Under dusty olive trees, armed rebels congregate for a smoke, oblivious to the battles they had fought that day. I turn another corner and pick up the pace, just in case.

The sun blows one last mean glow over everything. A Fanta sign sways in the breeze. The shop underneath is shuttered, save for a small opening at the bottom. I knock, hoping to find a place to hide. I collect my breath, because in a place like this, you can't be wearing your fear like a badge.

"Who are you?" the shopkeeper demands.

"I need food and water," I say, as if this is my only problem in life.

He pulls the metal shutter high enough for me to fold myself in, then he shoves it down again with a metallic roar that aggravates my budding headache.

The shopkeeper is all height and bulk. He wears a dark blue working overcoat that's tight at the seams and faded at the pockets. Decades of haggling have carved deep creases of discontent in his face.

Inside, a skinny boy and girl are huddled around a shortwave radio.

"What happened?" I ask the grocer.

"Nobody know," he says.

"Does everybody have it? Everywhere?"

The shopkeeper nods. If everybody has it, it'll change everything. That much is certain. The grocer points to a chair, then hands me a glass of water that I can barely hold. He sees it too, the tremor in my hands. Maybe it's shock. Or maybe I just need a cigarette.

From a rusting refrigerator, the grocer pulls out a cold Fanta and pops the cap for me. He asks his son to go fetch me some food. The sweet cold soda soothes my nerves, but I have no recollection of ever tasting it before. That's when it hits me, that my entire life has been completely deleted from existence—from my first Fanta to my last kiss. I no longer know where I live, whether I have a wife and children waiting for me back home. A wave of panic takes hold of me. I try to convince myself that I haven't lost everything. I list the things I do remember: the war; chemical weapons; how to work a video camera. All impersonal memories. What a waste if we're only left with the sterile facts.

I have a bad feeling that whatever did this to us can also kill us. I need to get over my confusion, my fear, understand what this is.

Just then someone bangs on the metal shutter with the butt of a gun, making the whole thing clatter. With trembling fingers, I finish my Fanta, like this has nothing to do with me. The grocer shouts something back, but thankfully doesn't open the shutter.

This might be the best time to hit the road, while both camps are trying to make sense of the fighting, the wounded, and the dead.

"I need to go home," I say, even though I have no idea where home is. "What town is this?"

The grocer unfolds an old map, with Idlib circled in red. Turkey doesn't look too far.

"Is it safe to cross the border?" I ask.

He winces. "Landmines."

I seem to know this too: the military buried landmines en route to the border, to punish fleeing refugees. There may be tricky checkpoints too.

"Can you stock me up for the crossing?" I pat the pockets of my cargo pants. Stray coins, but no bills. How embarrassing if I can't pay the guy.

I take one last look at the clunky Swiss watch on my wrist: expensive instruments under immaculate glass, dutifully rotating in three time zones. I remove it and set it on the counter. The shopkeeper asks no questions.

In an old pillowcase, he stuffs old plastic bottles filled with questionable tap water, dry-roasted chickpeas, his tattered map, a cheap compass, and a flashlight. When I ask for aspirin and cigarettes, he carefully wraps two pills and two loose smokes in a scrap of used notebook paper.

The boy hands me flatbreads warmed up in olive oil, and black olives bunched up in cloth. Ah, this makes me happy. I shake the kid's hand. He reminds me of the dead boy I filmed. It is the daughter who brings me a small blanket. It has her same smell, a combination of wool and soap, the kind made at home from rancid frying oil. She's young and thin like a blade of grass. When her father heaves the metal shutter open, she gives me the faintest smile before I step into the failing light.

I duck into the ancient olive groves surrounding the town, and keep heading northwest through the darkening scrubby landscape. Chomping on the salty olives and flatbread settles my stomach, but something is definitely wrong with me. Even after a cigarette and two aspirin, my headache continues to expand like an oil slick. The uphill walking in the tilled dry soil reveals a dull throb in one knee.

As for my mind, it holds cold, suspended facts, but it's devoid of people. With no memory of anyone in my life, my solitude feels infinite. If this amnesia erased all those we cherished, then it obliterated love itself from the face of the earth. I invent an imaginary girlfriend for myself. All I know is that I'm a war correspondent with a French accent. I have no name, no home, no family, no money, no past. What is a man without his memories? A kind of child. It's unnerving.

Through the mountainous border terrain, under the weak glow of the flashlight, I study the earth before me for signs of landmines. It makes for a slow, agonizing trek. I just have to accept that every step I take could be my last—after all, that is life itself. Walking through the night would be wise, to stay cool and invisible. But my body gives out too soon. When I clear the ground behind a shrub, a scorpion scurries away, its carapace a sickly yellow under the flashlight.

I shiver the entire night, in the rocky hills of Syria or Turkey, I'm not sure which, my thin sleep interspersed with the dead boy's face. But for the stars staring down, the darkness on the ground is absolute, teeming with hidden creatures.

There's only one good thing about this frigid, stony landscape. Here, there are no screams of despair; no human flesh ripped apart by bullets; no stench of corpses left to rot in the sun. At least not for now.

4

Chen

Finally the alarm stops, but the two cops keep yakking loudly. I pretend to wake up, and slowly raise my hands over my head.

"Come on, man, I didn't do a thing," I say, as one opens the door of my vehicle and the other one points a gun at me.

"Yeah, what about the Beemer going off?" says the mean cop, who's been on the job too long to stay nice. He looks the part too: underfed, worried, worn out. The other officer is softer-looking, like he's had a nice American childhood, with pancakes, soccer, and bedtime stories.

"Didn't touch it," I say. "I can't remember where I live, man. I have a right to sleep in my car."

"You didn't see the sign?" He points to the nearest pole.

Big red letters: no parking overnight. Douchebags have to remember all the complicated parking rules no one can figure out even when their head's working straight.

"Driver's license and registration," he says.

I hand him the license in my wallet. I don't make a move for the registration, 'cause I'm not real sure this rickety thing isn't stolen.

"Alec Chen," he says, "as in smart Alec?"

"Yeah, that's it." I roll my eyes.

"Alec's a funny name for an Asian," he says.

"Ha, ha," I say.

He checks the system then gets back to me.

"You're on parole in Massachusetts. Whatcha doing here in L.A.?"

People's brains got wiped and he cares about parole. I try the first thing that comes to mind, 'cause if you're gonna lie, you've gotta do it fast.

"Sister's wedding. I got permission," I say, looking at him without blinking.

"You'd better not dick around here, or we'll ship you right back to the polar vortex you came from."

His buddy looks over his shoulder at whatever they've found in my record. I really wanna find out myself, but this isn't the best time to be curious about your past crimes.

"Wasn't there a red Hyundai on the alerts with some kidnapped girl?" says one of them.

They're coming up with something just to search my car.

"Yeah, I saw it too. Worth a look."

"I'll take a look in the trunk, in case that girl's in there."

"What girl?" I say, horrified. "I ain't got no girl."

"Mind if we look in the trunk?" asks pancake boy, already walking back.

I have no idea what's in the stinking trunk of this car. I sure hope it's not a gagged kid—or a dead one. Joe releases the ancient lever and the trunk creaks open.

"Will ya come take a look at this shit?" says pancake boy.

Joe walks over. "What's this you got in here?"

"I don't remember," I squeak.

"That's what they've all been saying all day," says mama's boy.

"It's the fucking truth, that's why," I say.

They force me to take a look. Just the thought of a dead kid makes me queasy. I walk over, my hands up, hoping the wad doesn't slip out of my pocket. That's when I realize they forgot to pat me down.

"So? What the hell is it?" asks Joe, swinging a big flashlight around.

The red velvet upholstery lining the trunk reminds me of a Mexican coffin. It makes me ill. Then his flashlight shines on ten bottles of booze, neatly tucked into plastic holders that are stitched into the lining.

I'm so relieved it's not some kid that I crack up.

"It's a personal bar, that's what."

"Very funny." The junior one turns to his partner. "You think it's legal?"

"As long as there are no open containers in the car."

Joe walks back to the cabin of the Hyundai, yanking the doors open and flashing his nasty light all over. If he finds the rest of the cash, I'm dead meat.

Pancake boy eases a Jameson out of one sleeve, unscrews the top, sniffs, then hands it to me.

"Drink up. I want to make sure it's booze."

"You're not gonna give me a DUI for this, are you?"

"Just a sip," he says.

I take a slug. "Whoa, it's whiskey all right."

He sticks it back in the sleeve and slaps the trunk closed.

"Find anything in the cabin, Joe?"

I'm freaking out.

"Car's clean." Joe has a strange smile on his famished face. "All right, get going, Mr. Chen. Stay away from the Beemers next time. We have bigger fish to fry tonight."

I don't like this guy. I throw the car into drive and gently ease out into the street. I'm not real sure I remember how to drive, but I've got to beat it, before they change their minds. It's like driving dead stoned is what. We're in for some big trouble if everybody is driving this bad. A coupla blocks down the road, I pull over in a dark alley to check on the cash. I stick my fingers in the dark underbelly of the car seats and run through every nook and cranny, scratching my hands on the metal innards.

Nada. That fucking parasite snatched all four wads. He probably kept them for himself too. I'm pissed as hell, but what can I do, cry and file a complaint with internal affairs? Even the cops didn't forget how to nick someone's hard-earned dough. I guess all the bad habits survived the wipe-out.

Anyways, I gotta look on the bright side. At least they didn't pat me down, clean me out, then take me to the slammer. I've got one wad left on me.

Back on the road, there are traffic jams everywhere you look. I'm gonna use up all my gas sitting here. Not like I have a home to go to or a place to be, since I can't remember why I'm in L.A. in the first place—other than the small trip to the bank. Several blocks down, I spot a Motel 6 on Santa Monica Boulevard, across from the 7 Eleven. I'm gonna get myself a room, kick back, and lie low, in case the cops get the hint about where I got the cash.

I feel a lot better after finishing off the rest of the Jameson. On TV, there's mayhem everywhere: accidents, parents fighting over kids, stray dogs roaming around, alarms going off. Cops are in over their heads, so the national guard has been called in too. Folks out there are still all sniffly about their confusion. As for me, I'm starting to dig being whoever the fuck I wanna be. Who needs to remember their past anyways—especially if it included time in the lock-up? The past is way overrated—including all the unmemorable people in it. When you look at the mess out there, I'm doing all right. I've got a full tank of gas, a trunkful of booze, and a small pile of cash—instead of getting arrested. This memory loss thing seems to be made just for me. I don't remember much, but something tells me I'm a pro at all this shit. Everybody is trying to remember their line of business. I'm no exception.

An average Asian with an American accent. There's gotta be an edge somewhere. Maybe it's not my cunning or my pluck that's my lucky strike, but the fact that I look nothing like the crook I am. A short, skinny Asian with young genes, I can easily pass for a pharmacist, computer geek, or even the teenage kid next door. Because I'm neither ugly nor good-looking, I can fade away in any police lineup. I'm gonna hang underground for a while, till I figure out a way to exploit the situation.

5

Max

I wake up in the fragile light of dawn, only the rustle of animals in the air. For a moment, I'm hopeful. But the amnesia is still there, taking my whole life hostage—except for the day before. Yesterday is still mine to own.

While pulling my boots back on, I feel something lodged under the leather insole. It takes some digging and scratching to yank the thing loose: it's a warped US passport. I'm so happy, I kiss the stinky thing. I stare at the picture of a fellow with sepia eyes. He has a small-boned frame, and a fine dimple on his chin. His ruffled hair threatens to form a dark curtain over his face. I just hope it's me. "Maximilien Cattelain," I murmur. The name feels awkward, like borrowed shoes. But I'll take it. Any name is better than none at all.

The travel document is plastered with stamps from war-torn hotspots—Syria, Iraq, Afghanistan, Nigeria. This Max has been to them all. I was apparently born in Nice, France, twenty-nine years ago. Inside the flap is a handwritten address in Santa Monica, California. I don't know why, but I dread the place. Wedged inside the passport, I find a receipt for a frozen pizza from a 7 Eleven. On the back is scribbled: Sylvia Wright, Tuesday 4 p.m. The name means nothing to me. I wonder who this woman is.

~

After three days trudging through sun-blasted scrub with only the sound of crickets, I don't know if I'm delirious because of heatstroke, thirst, or some other big problem. With half a bottle of water to my name, my fate is in the hands of a five-dollar compass.

I finally see a drooping flag. It's an unmanned border crossing. By the time I hit the road in Turkey, I'm a sweaty, sunburned, disheveled mess with a dirty pillowcase on my back. For hours, I walk by the road—until a truck driver agrees to take me to the Antakya airport.

I catch my reflection in the truck's long side mirror. My face looks totally unfamiliar. It feels like someone else's face had been transplanted onto mine. I turn away from the horror of it. But then I glance back—and mentally compare it to the picture in the passport, because I'm not so sure they're the same man. The passport was issued only a year ago to a man with a smiling dimple and the optimistic confidence of youth. Yet the guy staring back looks like his older brother who'd just returned from hell. It's not just the grime from the trek. In such a short time, I must have lost twenty pounds, gained twenty years—and sold half my soul.

In the airport restroom, I wash up as best I can to try to look like my passport picture. The sticker on that video camera is my only hope, so I plead with the Turkish Airlines ticket agent to allow me to call the *New York Times* collect. I finally get a Melinda on the phone.

Melinda has a soothing Southern drawl, her words dripping with honey, sugar, and sweet nothings. It's so not New York that I wonder if I've dialed the wrong area code.

"I'm so glad you're alive, sweet pea. I was so worried about you," she says.

"How did you remember me?" I say, astonished.

"I keep a rolling list of our reporters out on assignment —so I know if you didn't come back and where to find you."

She's the first person to recognize me—it brings tears to my eyes. She pours out the company credit card number like fine bourbon, and even pre-pays some airport vouchers for meals and sundries. I want to keep talking to her, ask her what she knows about me, but there's a line of unhappy people behind me.

The ticket agent hands me boarding passes to L.A., but warns me they're still looking for a pilot for my plane. Not a good sign when the pilots themselves don't want to fly. Next stop is the news stand, where I buy a stash of newsprint, including old papers sold for five times the price. Sitting with Turkish coffee and a kebab, I become a news junkie all over again. The skinny papers of the last few days are full of crippled cities, long lines at hospitals, and presidents hiding in bunkers. Now that the chaos has been amply documented and photographed, journalists have turned to interviewing the few memory experts who remember that they have an expertise.

A fellow hovers around the tables, looking for a place to sit, a mounded plate of rice and kebabs in hand. He's wearing a Doctors Without Borders pin, and looks just as exhausted, disheveled, and hungry.

"Sit over here, if you can tolerate the stench," I say. "No showers on the trek over from Syria."

"No worries, mate," he says, sitting down at my table. "Comes with the job doesn't it?"

He's a British doc, who was volunteering at a refugee camp in Turkey when the amnesia hit.

"We were in theatre, operating on a kid with a gunshot wound—and then all of sudden none of us knew what we were doing there," he tells me in between bites. "Good thing we still knew how to stitch things back up. Habitual, I suppose. The entire camp descended on the clinic, convinced they all had a medical problem."

"Is it an epidemic?" I ask.

"Pandemic, yes," he says. "But no signs of infection so far. Too fast even for an airborne pathogen."

"Any idea of cause?"

"Whatever it is, it's bad news. Our memories are usually safe inside our skulls." He fills me in about what they know at this point, almost four days into it. "We're just not seeing the usual causes of amnesia. No mass head injuries, strokes, or encephalitis. Brain scans show no gross tissue damage."

"Is anybody immune?"

"It's hitting everybody. No exceptions," he says.

"Permanent?"

"Too early to know. So far, nobody's recovered."

"How come I remember how to work my camera, but nothing about my life?" I ask.

"It's what we call an autobiographical amnesia. It only affects memories of what we actually experienced: child-hood, school, marriage, that sort of thing. We just have never seen amnesia on a mass scale before."

"But how come I remember Assad but not if I have a wife?"

"General knowledge is stored in a different memory

center. Same with language. Same with muscle and procedural memory—things we did habitually, like working a camera."

"You think we're all going to be even more stupid now?" I ask.

He laughs.

"I know it's hard to believe, but IQ appears intact," he says. "It's not the kind of amnesia that prevents us from learning new information. I just hope that what new memories we form won't be destroyed, you know, by another event."

"You mean another mass wipe-out?"

He nods.

This possibility didn't even occur to me.

"Can it actually get worse?" I ask.

"Well, theoretically, it could progress to total amnesia for all memories stored since birth: talking; reading; using tools," says the doctor as he chews on his last kebab. "But I'm sure that won't happen."

What he's describing would be the unravelling of civilization.

"What about you, see anything strange on the front lines?" he asks.

"You could say that." I remember the memory card still tucked in my sock, the soldiers acting a little off. "They're confused for five minutes, that's all."

The doctor shakes my hand, and runs off to catch his plane, leaving me hours to sift through my stack of newspapers. The uncertainty about what could still happen to us deepens my malaise.

The media machine has already coined the term 'Day of Forgetting,' now cited everywhere in the papers. Apparently, scientists have entertained all kinds of causal agents already. Because it happened everywhere at around the same time on October 20th, many suspect a far-reaching event from outer space. At this point, NASA is still hard-pressed to uncover any cosmic phenomenon that could have penetrated the Earth's atmosphere and caused so much generalized havoc. Satellites failed to detect electro-magnetic disturbances in the ionosphere, and there were no radio or wire line communication disruptions or unusual aurorae. NASA is not giving up though, as half the world is convinced it can only be an interstellar event from deep space. The other half believes it's an act of God, perhaps punishment for our collective sins. If God were trying to make a point, wouldn't He have known that it would be promptly forgotten? As for me, I don't like being forced to pick from two camps. That's how wars happen. There's always a third possibility, even if you have to invent one.

What intrigues me is that the amnesia struck more or less simultaneously across the globe. But some places must have been affected at least milliseconds before others. There must be an epicenter, a ground zero, or a patient zero. Even if a rogue gravitational wave whacked the entire planet, you'd think the closest part of the globe would suffer before the farthest. Surely, the national laboratories are looking into this. But nothing says a journalist can't sniff out the facts first.

My thoughts return to what the British doctor said, and the long lines at the hospitals. People all over the world assumed they had a medical emergency, overwhelming doctors and first responders. Everybody must have been calling their emergency services. Like all 911 calls, those very first amnesia-related calls are automatically recorded and time and date stamped. These precious datapoints could help us understand if the amnesia descended on certain locations first. It's only a thread of intuition, a mere scent, but I need something to focus on, if only to anchor my mind.

It's worth keeping the stash of old newspaper pulp for now, in case the amnesia strikes again. I locate a computer terminal at the airport. Can my fingers still navigate a keyboard? Closing my eyes, I type *New York Times* in the search bar. The habitual is not lost, just as the doc said. Melinda's email is easy to locate on the website, as she's the assistant to the chief editor. In the email, I thank her, but also ask her to request some 911 caller data on The Day, from however many American states she can. I'm about to sign off, then remember the memory card. Maybe my video could be a small contribution to the news train. It'll become stale if I wait too long. I copy the videoclip onto the email, adding that the last ten minutes were filmed in Syria, at the very moment of the memory loss.

It turns out to be the first day that commercial planes are allowed to take off. None of the passengers are convinced that the pilot truly remembers how to fly a plane. They're all either praying or drinking—or both. I'm more afraid of what awaits me at my destination. My gut feeling is vague but sinister.

6

Chen

Two days later, I come out of my motel room and head to Denny's for breakfast. I'm starving after a vending machine diet washed down with Jack Daniels. I order steak, onion rings, and a cold one. Beer is my coffee. My nerves need soothing, not slapping. I sit myself in front of the TV to see if the jokers at the top have anything else to say about the memory deal.

Reporters are really getting desperate if they're interviewing all kinds of people on the street about what they think caused the wipe-out. Nobody remembers a thing about their lives, but everybody has an opinion. Waste of airwaves. I wanna ask the waitress to change the channel, but she looks so ditzy, it's a miracle she showed up for work. I walk over to the TV and figure out a way to change the channel myself.

On the BBC, they're interviewing some young memory

bigwig out of London who has grandpa hair and talks like Shakespeare.

"Why have we only forgotten our personal experiences, our past—but not our knowledge?" asks the reporter.

"It has to do with the hippocampus, the part of the brain that records autobiographical memories. It's also one of the most sensitive areas of the brain. For instance, we know it's the first part to get damaged by oxygen deprivation."

"Did something happen to the oxygen level?" asks the reporter.

"We haven't registered any dips in oxygen—but we're still looking through atmospheric data."

"And has anybody suddenly remembered their lives?"

"Some people have had better luck at reconstructing—not necessarily remembering—their pre-amnesia lives," says the professor. "So far, no one has demonstrated verifiable recall."

"Dr. Anderson, as someone who's experienced the amnesia yourself, do you have any advice for our listeners?"

"We must verify everything we uncover about our lives, because right now, we are at risk of confabulation, of filling the blanks with false information."

"Tell us more about confabulation," says the reporter.

"There is a memory vacuum, as it were, which our brain literally fills by inventing—or readily accepting—plausible information about ourselves and the world. As a result, we may latch onto wrong facts and accept falsehoods people tell us," says the professor dude.

My ears perk up. Huh?

"Amnesia makes us more suggestible to false information—and more impulsive too. If we are not careful, confabulation could be the long shadow of amnesia."

Those nerds, man, they come up with big words to make up for their small dicks. Confabulation is just a snooty way to say folks will believe the lies thrown at them. It can't get any better than this. The memory man on TV inspires me to go sit my ass down at the motel desk like a real working person and plan my next big move. If I was able to rob a bank with half a brain, then I should be able to do a bigger job with everybody still bumbling around.

Back in my room, I start scribbling on my free pad, not sure what'll come out, 'cause I sure don't remember a lick of school. I'm itching to be in on some big-time action. What's left of the bank money will soon run out, between the motel, food, booze, and gas. That much I know.

The stock market, banks, and casinos are all in lockdown, but the busy bees are inside getting things straightened out. Maybe I can show up somewhere, and say I lost my badge. With all the confusion, they might hand me a replacement ID as a cashier at Harrah's, or even as a security guard at Tiffany's or the Wells Fargo vault.

There's a big problem with cashiers though: they have cameras glued on them every stinking minute of the day. As for security guards at banks, casinos, and jewelers, they don't get to touch any of the cash or valuables. There's gotta be a better idea.

What about museum guards? They get to hang around the expensive artwork up close and personal. If I can finagle my way into one of those prissy museum jobs, I can study the situation, the cameras, the artwork, and set up a plan to get something small but pricy out of there, something I can sell on the black market for loads of cash—hopefully, enough to retire someplace like Thailand, where a crook can live like a King. Yeah, that's the spirit. Forget the small stuff. Aim high for a change. And if that memory nerd is right, this is the time to do this kind of junk, when people will believe any goddamn thing coming out of my mouth.

On my free pad, I write: "Get Job. Get Art. Sell Art. Fly Away Baby." That's enough to break a sweat. Now it's time to crack open another brew.

7

———

Max

In the foggy morning hours, I finally arrive at the Santa Monica address on my passport. No one answers the door. With my keys left behind in Syria, I have no choice but to ask the first tenant I see to call the building manager—then wait around for him.

Inside is a disappointment. This is not a home. This is the cave of a solitary animal. So much for my imaginary girlfriend. No woman would even spend the night in this sad studio, with its anemic light, layers of dust, and black rooftop for a view. I look around, hoping to learn something about myself. The bare walls stare at me, defiant. There are no mementos of my past here—not one photograph. All I find are bank statements and nondescript bills, including one from that Sylvia Wright, who knows for what service. Somebody with this kind of apartment either has something to hide or is hiding from something. It makes me nervous. Was I a CIA agent with a fake press badge? I swear, the walls keep laughing at me, inching closer. I'm really losing it. I take a hot shower and collapse on the bed, hoping sleep will cure whatever insanity is gripping me. But sleep does not visit a troubled mind. I'm convinced that the ceiling is plotting to crush me any moment. Could the amnesia be making me more mad with each passing day? Surely a man can't live in the present alone. The past is an anchor for the present—and a foil for the future.

An omelet would be good right now, but I'm suspicious of anything in the fridge. I settle on dry cookies dunked in coffee, when I spot a laptop on the top shelf. I'm hoping it contains clues to my life, but it's a work computer, devoid of personal data. There are hundreds of people in my email directory. In a normal world, I'd start with my mother, since everybody has one. There isn't a single other Cattelain in here, so how do I know which of these women is my mother? I search the internet for Cattelain in Nice, France. There is a whole tribe of them. I'd have to call them all to find out if we're related. Forget it.

In my inbox I find several emails from Melinda. She thanks me for my video, and informs me that they've posted it on the *New York Times* website. In an email 24 hours later, she tells me that it's going viral, that simple clip of the soldier trying to save the same kid he didn't remember shooting. It garnered some two million viewers in the time I'd been travelling. It helps that right now, everybody is eating up the news for breakfast, lunch, and dinner. Maybe I have a rat's nose for a good story.

Melinda also emailed me a link and codes to access datasets from the States of New York, Virginia, and Florida. The digital audio recordings of 911 calls on The Day are unlabeled, unsorted, other than by chronological order and county. The gigantic data files must hold some small secret about who lost their memory first.

I start working on it immediately, if only to distract my mind from the nonsense. To pinpoint the exact onset of the first amnesia calls in every county, I'm stuck listening to some thirty to fifty emergency calls. The calls right before the memory loss are filled with terror, horrific accidents and crimes. Right after the amnesia, callers are suspended in a mental vacuum, in free fall over the abyss that their lives have become. Listening to all these human catastrophes unfolding is demoralizing. There's no demographic group that stands out in the early amnesia callers. Like death, the amnesia doesn't spare anyone. The first amnesia-related calls in most New York and Virginia counties were all within the same minute. So for both states, I tabulate the exact onset time—to the second—of the first bellwether amnesia-related call in each county. To each narrow range of onset times, I assign a color, then map them. It takes a lot of cigarettes, bad coffee, and gum.

When I'm done, something strangely beautiful and perfectly menacing glares back at me from the computer screen: a pattern.

8

Max

The pattern is too systematic across both states to be a fluke —but is it something worthwhile? I know I have to replicate the pattern in Florida, and also somewhere other than the East Coast before informing our chief editor. I forgot to eat again.

I want to open the fridge to see what I can find in there. But I can't seem to shake the conviction that there's a dead body inside. This is more than amnesia: something is just not normal in my head. I finally give in and call the neighborhood medical clinic.

The young internist is a stunning brunette with incredible Zen, considering her waiting room full of agitated people. Dr. Rani looks depleted from attending to the hundreds of real and imagined crises. People are still turning to medicine like the amnesia is a medical ailment with a cure, when doctors are just as burdened by their own personal lives in shambles. Perhaps it's not so much a medical problem, as an existential one. After all, there have been few deaths despite the chaos.

It's hard not to stare at Dr. Rani's hypnotic eyes, slender neck, and the bronze afterglow of her skin. Reluctantly, I tell her about the strange symptoms that are getting worse by the day: the headaches, aches, nausea, and the feeling that something is out to harm me.

While she checks my pulse and palpates my neck, I bask in Dr. Rani's attentions. As clinical as it is, it's the first human touch I can remember—and it is fabulous. Closing my eyes, I relish the flutter of her hands as she listens to my lungs. Her scent is a mélange of bergamot, alcohol swabs, and latex. She asks me to lie down to check my abdomen. While she kneads my gut, I remind myself that I'm naked underneath the medical gown. I turn away from her, and stare at the cheap plastic art.

Her gloved fingers gently tickle my forearm.

"You use drugs?" she asks.

"Of course not," I say, offended.

"How about before the memory loss?" She dabs at the crease of my left arm, speckled with blue and red puncture marks. "We see these in intravenous drug users."

Merde. That hypodermic needle in my backpack, which I thought was just part of a smart traveler's medical kit, was something else entirely.

Dr. Rani snaps off her gloves, and tells me that my physical symptoms and paranoia are consistent with a bad case of opioid withdrawal.

"How can this be?" I protest.

"Maybe you forgot you were dependent on something," she says softly. "People forgot all kinds of things, including life-saving medications." She sees my growing shame and her eyes soften. She puts her left hand on my shoulder, a hand without a ring. "I forgot my profession until I saw my lab coat."

I can't resist. "You also forgot you're my girlfriend," I say.

"Nice try." She smiles and gives me what looks like a second glance. But I'm dreaming. There's no way she'd be interested in me. I'm apparently an addict now. I maneuver the conversation away from drugs.

"Could it be a virus attacking our brain?"

"I almost wish, because at least we know something about viruses and have some tools against them," she says.

"What's your best guess?" I try to prolong the conversation amongst equals, pull us out of our scripted roles.

"Only a cosmic event could do this to all of us at once." She tells me that even the astronauts on the international space station have the amnesia, and they weren't breathing the same air.

Trying to hold my own, I remind Dr. Rani that NASA has ruled out sun flares, coronal mass ejections, geomagnetic storms—and that there's no evidence that our memories are sensitive to cosmic events.

"Unless it's a completely novel one," she says. "The human species is young—it may not have encountered all possible cosmic events out there."

I know the news inside out, but she has the medical degree.

"Is there anybody who doesn't have it?"

"Not yet." She tells me she's required to report anybody with an intact memory to the Centers for Disease Control and Prevention. We both laugh at the irony of referring perfectly healthy people for further study. "All right, Max the journalist, interview over. Let's leave the cause of amnesia to the memory experts, and let's focus on your health. Find any drugs or paraphernalia?"

I fess up to the unused syringe in my travel kit. She congratulates me for forgetting to shoot up.

"Maybe you'd just started using and it's not yet habitual."

Maybe. I read over her shoulder: she's checking off a slew of blood tests on a form, including HIV and Hepatitis C. More hurdles. I shift in my floral gown.

She hands me a prescription for a mild opioid replacement to tone down the withdrawal, and a sample with several starter pills.

"Don't mix methadone with street drugs—and no alcohol either. It can be lethal. If it's heroin, it's no joke." Her warm hand alights on my shoulder again. "Right now, your body is in withdrawal, but your mind has forgotten your habit. This is a good opportunity to kick it."

I promise her that I'll never touch drugs again, then ask her to check my knee.

"Have you over-exerted it lately?"

"A bit of hiking in the Middle East," I say.

Dr. Rani chuckles then leans down to inspect it. As she bends over, the curves underneath her lab coat stir me again. Flexed, my knee is even more painful.

"Sorry. We'll need x-rays on this one." She signs another order. "Amazing video by the way."

"What, you saw my video?" I can't believe she knows who I am outside the clinic. I thought I was just a patient tethered to a medical file. Nothing like flattery from someone you want to have sex with to make you feel better. As a newly minted attending, Dr. Rani knows how to use all her tools, from stethoscope to sex appeal.

"Your video shows that even war can be forgotten," she says. "Maybe there's something good in all this mess."

I give her a noncommittal smile. I can't buy that rubbish. My short clip makes for a nice story, but the rest of the footage proves the absolute contrary. I'm cheating people of the truth. A moment of confusion won't change human nature. One instant they forget who they are; the next, they see their weapons, their uniforms, and figure out which side they're on. I want to tell her that for some people, reloading and shooting is procedural, habitual, routine.

It's best not to share this with her though. If doctors knew what horrors their patients are capable of, they would never place a consoling hand on them. I'm really enjoying the conversation with her. If only I had the courage to ask Dr. Rani out on a date. But what doctor would go out with a junkie?

While Dr. Rani copies down a few telephone numbers from her computer screen, I notice a list of attending pager numbers taped on the desk. I memorize Rani's, just in case someday I'm feeling brave. She hands me the note.

"I want you to call one of these psychologists—they're all in the neighborhood, and have worked with our clinic before."

I'm about to object and tell her I'd rather see *her* for an hour every week, but then I see how serious she is. One of the names turns out to be familiar: Sylvia Wright is a shrink I must have seen before. Clearly, she hasn't cured me. I pocket the note.

"Call today. Tell them it's urgent," orders Dr. Rani. Then her voice softens. "Will you do that for me?"

"I will do that—for *you*," I say, amused.

Dr. Rani catches herself in a newbie's blunder. By stepping off the pedestal, she has made herself even more desirable. What the hell, luck has been on my side so far.

"Please, have dinner with me tonight," I say, taking her hand gently in mine.

"I'm very flattered, but you *are* my patient."

"Be my girlfriend instead. I'll find another doctor."

"It's not ethical," she says.

As if there aren't enough sins already, they have to invent new ones.

"People can't remember what wars they were fighting, and you think they care about us having a date?" I say. "Just meet me for dinner. It's the best thing you can do for me." I plant an unethical kiss on her hand.

She's speechless. In America, women know only an extraterrestrial would kiss their hand. Dr. Rani doesn't say yes or no. She can't help but smile, then leaves the room in a hurry, before something worse happens.

I stand there in my floral gown, happy for the first time since the amnesia.

Still, maybe I shouldn't have been so forward with her.

I walk out of the clinic with more problems than when I came in. This is why people dread going to the doctor. Now I have a drug problem *and* I'm in love with my internist. If I find a way to impress her, maybe she'll give me a chance. But she's that upwardly mobile immigrant woman who has completely internalized Western political correctness, may it rot in hell. Plus, I'm sure a whole legion of doctors has been trying to seduce her. I'd have to do something extraordinary to show her that I'm a Clint Eastwood type who can confront life without any crutches. That won't be easy for me.

So she found my work on the battlefield impressive enough to click on—but clearly not enough to go out with me. I don't even know much about her, because all we talked about was the amnesia, the wretched news. Maybe she'd be impressed if I somehow broke the story about what caused the memory loss. But maybe not. She's the type to admire the scientist who discovers the cause more than the reporter who first brings the story to the world.

If at least I were an investigative reporter who tracks epidemics. But I'm only good at filming people killing and people dying. Those investigative reporter types sift through mountains of data until they uncover a tiny grain of truth. I have no such patience. I'm a hunter, not a gatherer; a jackal, not an ant. Still, maybe I could sniff out something big from those 911 calls if I spent more time on them. I would do it for Rani.

It takes all of five minutes to convince myself that if only I unearthed the cause of the memory loss, Rani would fall in love with me. She would no longer see me as a hopeless rehab patient, but as a real man. Of course, it's irrational and childish. But in that moment, my passion feels boundless.

9

Max

Energized by my new muse and the nice pill she gave me, I go back to my computer, and try to find a way to tame the Florida data into something coherent. So far South, Florida would give us a nice contrast. But Florida is a populous state, and it's taking forever. I email Melinda, and beg her to obtain more data from as many states as possible, as well as Canada and Mexico. I decide to finish the Florida calls after some real dinner. On the way out of the lobby, I come across the mailboxes. Mine is stuffed solid.

Seated at an eatery nearby, I start slitting envelopes open, disgorging them of their kernel of news.

Prior to The Day, Melinda forwarded me stashes of fan mail—and hate mail—related to a piece I had written about the factions in Syria, accompanied by a short video. People can love and hate the same thing with equal intensity.

Amongst the neglected bills, an envelope catches my eye. It bears the seal of the State of California. I rip into it, expecting the state's inevitable demand of time or money: jury duty, taxes, or a speeding ticket. Instead, what I unfold in my cold fingers is a death certificate.

I flinch. The death occurred some five months ago. The name is Josephine Dupont. Nowhere is any mention of her relationship to me. The cover letter just refers to 'your loss,' which, in California, can easily apply to a pet. The official apologizes for the delay in issuing the certificate, which 'we hope you understand, given the unusual circumstances of the death.' What unusual circumstances? The cause of death is listed as 'unknown.' How can they not know? My eyes locate the two digits printed beside 'age.' Josephine Dupont was twenty-seven years old when she died. Who was this woman? There's only one quick way to find out. In my phone's search bar, I type Josephine Dupont.

There are hundreds, thousands with the name.

It feels like a gaping crater opened up in my life—but it fails to engulf me just yet. I manage to get up, collect my mail, and walk away. I must find out who Josephine is and how she died. If this Sylvia Wright was truly my therapist before the amnesia, she would have notes that might tell me who Josephine was and what happened to her.

There will be no sleep tonight.

10

Chen

A search for Alec Chen on a criminal background website tells me I just finished doin' time for some nasty shit I don't want to know more about. What's the point in torturing yourself, man? That was the old Chen, and I don't even know that guy. All it means is that I need to get my hands on a fresh ID.

I figure the waiting room of the county mental health clinic is the perfect place. It's full of lost souls who're waiting around for services that aren't coming. Chances are most of these guys have a clean record 'cause you've got to have your wits about you to be a crook. I show up to the neighborhood clinic in Santa Monica. After scribbling a fake name on the list, I go sit on a seventies couch that's a guaranteed bedbug residence. I try to look just kooky enough to blend in.

A few people walk in, but nobody sits near me. Maybe I've overdone it.

I'm about to call it quits and try another branch, when a

sorry-looking dude sits right next to me. Overweight white guy, wearing hand-me-downs. He's not lookin' too happy. He's telling an invisible woman to beat it, shooing her away. I pull out the old magazine from under my chair. It's a Hustler I brought along for the occasion, folded strategically so it displays the centerfold in a compromising position.

I thrust the magazine in the guy's hands.

"You drop this?" I say.

The fellow leans over the glossy, confused, trying to make sense of what body part he's looking at exactly. I'm about to pinch his wallet from his pant pocket, when a door opens and a lady blares out a name. Why the hell did she do that for? The guy looks startled, then walks up to her like a lost puppy, and tells her he's the guy she called.

Darn it. I make for the door and disappear into a side street. Now I'm gonna have to find some other lost soul. The city must be full of them.

11

Max

The only view from Dr. Sylvia Wright's office is of a halfway house across the street. On her wall is a brand new psychologist's license just issued last year, with a golden seal that's a tad too shiny for comfort. Sylvia has dark green eyes with pupils deep as wells, the pale patina of shock, and a straight black bob. She doesn't appear to be weathering the amnesia that much better than me.

"Can you help me remember who I am?" I ask.

The question startles her.

"I can try," she says.

"Do you think the amnesia is psychological?" I ask.

"Psychogenic amnesias can happen—say after a trauma —but we've never seen a collective type," she says.

"I know I came here before, because I found a bill from you. Why did I come here before the amnesia?" I ask.

"What's more important is why you're coming in now," she says, deflecting my question.

I tell her about the heroin habit I 'discovered' after the amnesia.

"Was Dr. Rani the one who referred me to you before the amnesia?" I'm curious if I had known Rani beforehand.

"My notes say you were referred by a different doctor, from the same clinic," she tells me.

"Well, I managed to fall in love with her in the time it took her to write your telephone number." I force a chuckle. "Does the amnesia make people fall in love more easily?"

"Yes, I think it makes us more impulsive."

"Maybe it's better that way," I say.

"Maybe. Is there something that might have triggered your dependence on heroin?" She's trying to be matter-of-fact, to glean what I already know about my past.

"This was in my mailbox." I hand her the death certificate, my hands trembling. "I want to know who this Josephine is and how she died," I say point blank.

I see the self-doubt flicker in her eyes, as though she was expecting the question—and dreading it. She says nothing.

"Who is she?" I prompt.

"I'm sorry, Max. She was your wife."

I knew there was a deep crater in my life. I could feel it. I should be feeling more pain, but strangely, I don't.

"What else is in your notes?" I ask, bracing myself.

Part of me is dying to know, but the other part doesn't want to know any of it. These opposing forces will spar over it for a while. Sylvia is picking her words wisely, hoping they don't explode.

"What I had written in my notes will not help you. It will only hurt you more," she says.

"Please, my ignorance is killing me. How did she die?"

"It's best to set it aside for now."

"And let my wife die forgotten, without even visiting her grave?" I say, perhaps too loudly.

46

Sylvia bites her lip, then says, slowly, softly, "She has no grave, Max. And no ashes either."

I fold over in a bundle. What horrible death that it would deprive me of a grave to cry on, or ashes to scatter.

"What happened to her?" I ask.

Sylvia scans her office window, like it's an escape hatch. Why is she withholding so much, and only releasing the information with a dropper?

"You're not answering my questions," I point out. "Isn't therapy all about bringing the hurt out in the open, instead of sweeping it under the rug?"

"That's the general idea, yes," she says, a bit miffed. "Look, you seem stronger today than before the amnesia. That's why it's best to wait before revisiting your past, in case it reverses your progress."

I look down, confused by this.

"So I was even more of a basket case before the amnesia?"

"Not a basket case. You had PTSD."

"I see. Look, I just want to honor my wife."

"You honored her and grieved her to the point of self-destruction. I was your witness," she says. "You also punished yourself: heroin, risky war zones, including your most recent trip to Syria."

I absorb all this in silence.

"All this is in your notes?" I finally say.

She nods.

"Impressive," I say. "Well, I want a copy of your notes then."

She was not expecting this.

"Max, once you know your past, you'll never forget it."

I glance at the flimsy filing cabinet in the corner, knowing the record of my life with Josephine is locked away in there.

"I lost every single memory of Josephine. What more do I have to lose?" I say.

"Yourself, perhaps. The grief almost killed you. You had thrown away every reminder of your past, and walked into an unfurnished studio with only your passport—all to forget. Don't you see, it's as though the collective amnesia was made just for you?"

"I can't forget her," I say.

"You can. You have, this entire time, because of the amnesia. If it weren't for the death certificate, you wouldn't have asked about her. It's best not to know any more for now. Please."

I sigh, frustrated. PTSD doesn't sound like something I want to re-acquaint myself with any time soon.

"All right, I'll do it your way, but I still want my therapy notes," I say. "They're all I have. They're like her ashes. I need to have them."

It's her turn to sigh.

"On one condition," she says. "I'm placing them in a sealed envelope, so that if you ever do read them, we do it here, together."

"OK," I say.

That is the very reason the word OK exists—for situations like these.

12

Max

When Sylvia hands me the sealed envelope, she has a haunted look in her eyes, like she'll never see me again. She's scrolled her signature across the lip of the envelope, then taped over it, to discourage me from opening it.

By the time I leave her office, the cloudy autumn night has fallen early. Outside, the bright street lights sting my eyes. My wife, Josephine, age 27. Dead five months ago. Cause: Unknown. No grave, no ashes. An icy chill courses through me as I run through all the tragic possibilities that leave no body behind. Josephine drowned. She was swallowed by an avalanche. She was blown up in an explosion. She's in a mass grave. I don't really want to know. But my mind keeps coming up with more scenarios.

The dark crater is beckoning me. It's still hungry.

Sylvia means well. She's coaxing me away from the edge of the crater, which must be my tomb. I want to know who this woman was to me, see her picture, understand how she suffered in her final hours. Forgetting her feels like an insult, a betrayal, like burying her in oblivion.

The envelope in my vest pocket contains some four or five sheets of paper, but weighs on me like a mountain. This cold-hearted amnesia has left us scavenging the remains of our loved ones from death certificates and medical charts.

Everything hurts: my head, my knee, my heart—this heart that must have ripped open, but is strangely still beating. I no longer know the love of my life—but will forever miss her.

On this balmy evening, the Santa Monica musicians, clowns, and wannabe opera singers with their scratchy boom boxes are out in full force, making a circus of my despair. After the president begged everyone to go back to work, they all looked up their social media profiles, figured out who they were supposed to be, and stepped right back into their dance shoes and their Michael Jackson costumes. Following the amnesia, there are few tourists feeding the frenzy with their indiscriminate applause and furtive dollar bills, but growling stomachs don't give a damn about lost memories.

Maybe I too should go back to where I belong: the battlefield. As for tracking down the cause of the amnesia, how could I be so presumptuous?

I'm utterly dejected on these streets, artificially enlivened by the desperate talent shows under every street-light. I look away from the clowns.

As I turn the corner, some guy bumps into me. First thing I see are his shiny gold Nikes.

"Hey, watch your step," I say.

"You want any?" says the young Latino.

"Any what?"

"Anything you want. I got everything, bro."

I look at the kid. How could this high school drop-out just read it on my face, the explosive migraine, the deep pit in my life, the miles of solitude all around me?

For an instant, I vaguely remember what Dr. Rani said about the meds, her latexed fingers caressing my needle marks, as if she were trying to plug the holes. What was I thinking? She'll never go out with me.

Besides, I'm supposed to be mourning my dead wife. No matter that I can't remember anything about her, not one thing.

"Got any White Nurse?" I say. So my drug slang survived the amnesia.

"Yep, got it all," says the kid, leading me into a deserted alley.

I open my wallet and hand him the cash. The kid even throws in a free syringe. He's showing up to work prepared.

Rani is right, it's not yet an ingrained habit, because standing in a dark doorway, I struggle to find a good vein and work the plunger. I regret it as soon as I finally manage to inject the stuff. Then the stuff conveniently erases all regret. This is chemical amnesia. Temporary, but deeply satisfying while it lasts. The headache evaporates, the aches, the dullness, the paranoia—and everything else I thought was just part of my crabby personality. Soon I feel like I've injected myself with pure freedom.

It even comes with a bonus: inspiration. I want to get back on my computer, analyze more data, write a killer piece. I just need this one hit to access my creativity, I tell myself.

I don't even make it out of the alley before I come crashing down. I feel faint, ill. Maybe it's just a bad trip, tainted stuff. Or it's that I already had methadone on board. I can't seem to get enough air. I'm hyperventilating, my heart is racing. Breathing faster doesn't get me more oxygen. I'm suffocating, drowning in an imaginary sea.

Shit, I'm dying.

I didn't really want it to end so soon. There are still things I want to do. Please, just a few weeks, a few days. Please. Not yet. Not now.

13

Chen

As a consolation prize, I decide to pick up a six-pack on the way back to my motel. I take the shortcut through the alley to the 7 Eleven. The place stinks with piled up trash. Garbage boys conveniently forgot what they did for a living. There's even a bum passed out in the middle of the street. He's gonna get flattened if the dump truck ever comes around.

"Hey, man, ya really wanna get run over?" I nudge him with my shoe.

He doesn't move. He's cleaned up, huddled inside his wool coat, ashen and cold, like a man rescued from the Titanic. White people man, they can be so fucking white you can't even tell if they're ill or dead.

Something's poking out of his vest. An envelope with 'confidential' scrawled on it, and a prescription bottle. I glance around to make sure nobody's looking then check out the label on the pills. It's methadone, with his name on it—a Maximilien Cattelain. Poor bastard OD-ed. I drop the pills back in his pocket. I don't even wanna touch that shit. You can get addicted just looking at it. I'm about to bolt out of there, when I spot the guy's wallet in the same pocket. I leaf through it. Not much cash in there. One of those modern people who pay everything by text and email, and make it hard for the rest of us. Better to only snitch the driver's license, so it looks lost, not stolen. Feels lousy to steal a dying man's ID.

I turn the corner and duck into the convenience store.

"Hey, there's a guy passed out in your alley," I tell the Asian cashier lady. "You might wanna call an ambulance."

"Busy with customa," she barks in a thick Taiwanese accent. "You call 911."

She's helping some big biker dude load up on booze, like a dying man has to wait his turn in line too.

"Call 'em yourself, lady. I got no phone anyways." If I call those assholes, they're gonna blame me for it—and lock me up again.

The cashier lady pushes her clunky phone in my hand with a bossy glare, while the biker dude grins at me.

Can't believe I'm dialing up the cops, like they're my best buddies.

"Young man OD'ed in the alley behind the Seven Eleven, on Santa Monica Boulevard. Come and get him." I'm about to hang up when the dispatch lady asks me for my name. "What does it matter what my name is? I'm Guy On The Street, that's who."

"What's your phone number, sir?"

"I'm borrowing a phone just to call you, lady."

"And the victim's name, sir?"

"Who cares about his name? You got a list of people you save and people you don't? Just get your asses over here before he dies. Now buzz off."

I hang up and hand the phone back. Too many bitches and bastards on this planet—fucking amnesia didn't make anybody nice, that's for sure.

Nosy cops always wanna keep tabs on everybody. That's how innocent people get dragged to jail. I'd better scram out of here and buy my beer some other time, before they show up and find the dude's ID on me.

Back at the motel, I look at the driver's license. Maximilien Cattelain. Funny name, but it'll do. Sounds too much like Maxi pad. Still, it could be a good omen. Maximum Millions. Age twenty-nine—and dumping it down the drain already. I just hope Maxi has a cleaner record than mine, is all. I'm only a few years younger than him, but I look a decade younger. Asian genes that wanna live forever, I guess. Maybe if I grow a goatee, I'll look old enough. I just have to get the picture doctored 'cause my new buddy Maxi-Million is not even close to Asian.

14

Max

Someone is shining a bright light into my eye. I sit up, startled, and when my eyes adjust, I see a doctor in scrubs—and tubes coming in and out of my body.

"Well, you survived this one," he says with a scratchy voice. "You've got a good Samaritan to thank for calling 911. You might not be so lucky next time."

I vaguely remember what brought me to this hospital room. Merde.

"So, Mr. Max, why did you mix methadone and heroin?" His voice is both amused and stern, like I'd been playing in the sandbox with dynamite.

What can I possibly tell him? To feel better momentarily? Better to say nothing.

The physician goes through the motions of checking my lungs, heart, throat, his big hands rough on my skin. He tells me about the all-nighter extravaganza at the ER. I close my eyes, feeling naked in a bad way underneath yet another wretched hospital gown.

"Did you really want to hurt yourself, Max?"

Not to hurt myself, I want to tell him, but to end the hurt. It's a problem when the self and the hurt are inseparable. But I don't try to explain, because he's not the type to understand these things.

"Was it a new or used syringe?" he asks.

"It was in a packet." It's best not to tell him that the syringe came from the dealer kid, and that I was in too much of a hurry to care if the packet was sealed.

"Your blood work came out clean, by the way. Let's keep it that way." He removes the IV and the catheter without any delicacy. "X-ray showed hairline cracks in your patella. An impact injury to the kneecap. From a hard blunt object, maybe four to six months ago. Any idea from what?"

"Maybe an angry girlfriend," I say.

He takes me literally and doesn't smile.

"You need to take it easy, otherwise your knee will need surgery, yes?"

His pager goes off before I'm forced to agree with him.

"Anyway, I've got to take this, but the nurse will come finish up." He gives me a pitiful smile I can do without, then leaves.

My clothes are bundled in a plastic bag on the floor. I put them on and sit back on the examining table. I'm glad to find my wallet in my vest pocket. Everything looks in place, though my driver's license must have slipped out in the kerfuffle. In the other pocket is Sylvia's manila envelope, soiled, but still sealed. Look at that, I relapsed without even reading my tragic therapy notes. So what would I do to myself if I read about the horrors in my past? I'm no Clint Eastwood, that's for sure.

The washed-out imitation art hanging on the wall is

depressing, as if clinics can only afford garage sale rejects. There's not enough art or poetry in the world. After last night's chemical spree, my body sits heavy. A general exhaustion is claiming me when a lazy-eyed, African-American nurse barges in, startling me.

"If you sign here, we'll send your ER records to your primary care physician. Dr. Rani, right?"

Oh, God no. If Rani sees what I did, she'll never give me a chance.

"Actually, I have a different primary care doc now," I say, taking the blank form from her and pocketing it. "I'll fill out the release and give it to you later."

"Uh-huh. Well, then you're all set, Mr. Cattle'in." She makes my name sound like something to do with herding cows. "All you need to do is get some rest and follow doctor's orders." She holds the door open, in case I don't get the message.

That is a tall order indeed: take a pill; see a shrink; get over heroin; get over Rani; don't use dirty syringes; don't mix meds, and booze; be nice to your body; stop acting like a child; grow up into a law-abiding, self-respecting, politically correct automaton.

I'm lucky if I manage to do one of those things.

15

Max

All this talk of heroin makes my body, my head ache again. As I pass by dingy alleys, visions of syringes and snowy powder bark at me like rabid dogs. I run straight back home and swallow Dr. Rani's medication like a talisman.

Look at this empty apartment. Sylvia is right: I must have been intent on escaping my life with Josephine even before the memory loss, because there is absolutely no evidence of her in here. Maybe she's right about something else too, and I should listen to her: only a man who had thoroughly mourned his wife would get rid of all mementos of her. All this guesswork about my past leaves me exhausted. I need to do something drastic to catapult myself out of this emotional quagmire. What I really need is the only effective therapy I know of: to share a fine French meal with a smart and beautiful woman.

But Rani is a mirage. I don't even know her first name. She probably discovered by now that she has a long-lost boyfriend, some top-dog surgeon who's only addicted to narcissism, which is more socially acceptable than heroin.

I dial Rani's pager anyway, congratulating myself for memorizing it from the attending list.

"Dr. Rani here." Her tone is all business. She's ready for any human disaster.

"Will you have dinner with me tonight?" I say.

"How did you get my pager?"

"I'm not a stalker," I say. "I'm just a hopeless romantic. Please don't cure me."

I hear her smile on the other end.

"Max, I'm swamped. A lot of people need help right now."

"But doctors still have to eat, don't they?"

Before she hangs up, I manage to tell her that I'll be waiting for her at 7 p.m. tonight at Quatre Epingles, a French bistro I'd come across in between her clinic and my apartment. Rani doesn't say she'll be there, so I can only wish and hope and pray.

While I was busy getting myself into trouble, my guardian angel, Melinda, emailed me links to 911 dispatch audiofiles she'd managed to extract from seven other American states with liberal privacy laws—and Mexico. I'm ecstatic. I Skype her to thank her in person. She appears on my screen, in all her six-foot-two stature, her shiny black hair in a tidy bun, her chocolate arms smooth and comforting. So this is the woman who saved me at the Turkish airport.

"You're welcome, darlin'. Still working on getting you more."

How come I can't call her darling too? Melinda is a positive 'yes' person. She never says 'no' to any challenge. It's refreshing.

"How are you, little busy bee?" she asks, genuine concern in her eyes.

I wonder if my problems are written all over my pallid face. Can she tell that I escaped a war zone only to try my luck at dying in an alley? I need to stay professional, focus on something I do have control over.

"I might be onto something, but don't tell Brownell yet," I say about our managing editor.

"Now, sugar, you need to understand that You-Know-Who is going to want to know what you're up to at this point, so be prepared for a phone call, sweet pea." Her voice shifts down to a whisper. "Just a warning: he's in a nasty mood these days. The amnesia has completely messed up the news cycle and he's not happy about it." She's always taking care of me, like I'm a blind kitten without a mother. If Melinda weren't almost a foot taller than me, I'd have certainly married her.

Seven more hours before dinner. Maybe I can finish plugging in the Florida onset times, start on the new data, and hopefully coax some juicy news bite out of my map to impress Rani tonight—if she ever shows up. I attack the datasets immediately, hoping to duplicate that pattern I'd found on the East Coast. I have a method now. I have to work quickly, before Brownell gets on my case. He sounds tough to please.

The gorgeous pattern on the US-Mexico map smiles at me again. The first amnesia-related 911 calls occurred slightly later in Northern US states, slightly earlier in Southern states, and even earlier in Southern Mexico. There's no indication from these numbers as to why—and I have no idea what this means. The national laboratories must have discovered this small but reliable effect already— but the government is just not telling.

16

Max

I wait at Quatre Epingles bistro, not at all sure if Rani will make an appearance. She never said she would. I overhear the chef cussing like a French whore. I like this guy already. I ask the waiter if I can talk to the chef. Pascal comes around, his beefy hands dusty with flour, ready to take on the whiny patron who interrupted his cooking. When I introduce myself in French, he breaks into laughter. Pascal sits down at my table and orders a bottle of the best Cabernet on the house, unconcerned about customers waiting for their dinner.

Neither of us remembers much about our lives back in France. Even exchanging immigrant factoids, such as how long we've been in the US proves to be a challenge.

"I bet you've been here longer than me," says Pascal.

"How would you know?"

"Because you're skinnier. You must have been feeding on bad American food for many more years."

"That would make me fatter, not skinnier," I point out.

"My sister told me the mess is just as bad in France," says Pascal. "I forgot I had a sister, until I got an express package of black truffles from her."

"That's a sister worth remembering."

"What about your folks?" he says.

"No one called me. I must not be memorable." I chuckle, making light of it. I don't tell him that playing detective with my life has not been all that fun for me, since my past is not filled with nice sisters sending me gourmet care packages.

"You'll figure it out," says Pascal.

"So why do you think you came to America?" I ask.

"Surely to feed withering French expats like you," he says with a wink. "And you, why are you here?"

I try to think of something positive, and Melinda comes to mind.

"I think I'm here because America is the land of 'yes.' People say 'yes' here, then make it work. Americans also have an endearing way of convincing themselves that life is good—even during a global catastrophe."

"That's true. As for us, we could be on a four-week vacation in a chateau, enjoying a Michelin-star dinner, and still bitch about how rotten life has been in France."

Naturally, Pascal and I must bitch a little about those vexing American habits and customs, which, sadly, the amnesia has not taken away: waiters who whisk away your plate before you eat your last morsel; zero-fat dairy products that taste of wet plaster; or the fact that nobody knows how to bake a decent baguette in the entire fifty states.

"The French bakers who come to the US never made it in France," he says, "and they have the gall to blame American flour and water for their lousy product. If I blamed the butter and the poultry, it'll never end. Is someone joining you?" asks Pascal when he sees I haven't ordered yet.

"It depends on my luck." I shrug and raise an eyebrow.

"Here's to better luck with women," toasts Pascal. "Maybe this amnesia will make them forget their chastity belts."

"I doubt it."

"If they're still being mean, I have a whole cellar of *vin rouge*." He winks. "That's why the stuff was invented, you know," he says, before ducking back into his kitchen.

Indeed, that's how a real Frenchman poisons himself. Pascal would be appalled if he knew I had gotten high on something that isn't even tasty.

I finish my one glass of wine and then sip Perrier, like a school girl. I valiantly abstain from smoking, even if Pascal turns a blind eye to it around the fire pit in the courtyard. I don't want to do anything that would alienate the good doctor. Heroin is a bad enough habit, I reason; cigarettes could put her over the edge.

I'm on the verge of abdicating and lighting up, when Rani arrives. She's dressed in faded jeans and a shabby sweater that looks more like a bathmat, as if to make a statement that although she's not on the job, she's not on a date either. She could have showed up in a burkini for all I care, though I do appreciate the tight jeans.

"I won't stay long—just enough to make it clear that this isn't going to fly," she says.

"You could have made your point on the phone," I say.

"I tried."

"Why don't you at least have some dinner for all your trouble?"

At that, I make a secret signal to the head waiter, Olivier, who comes back instantly with warm gougères redirected from a patron who actually ordered them. The aroma of warm gruyère plays in my favor, as Rani sits down to avoid loitering between the crowded tables. The French waiter, ordinarily an expert at making his precious services rare, immediately rematerializes at our table to pour her a glass of Cabernet.

"Do I have permission to drink one glass with you?" I can't possibly count my first glass, as I'd drank that one with Pascal.

"One glass," she says.

More appetizers show up, followed by entrées and salads, without as much as a natural break when Rani can make a polite exit.

"Fast service here," she marvels.

Soon the wine softens her. She even plays with her shimmering dark locks once or twice, a telltale sign that she's shedding her invisible lab coat.

If it is a date at all, it is a rather tricky one. Exchanges about our past histories are practically impossible. So we limit our questions to the present, to our lives since the amnesia. This is perfectly fine with me.

She tells me how the memory loss has multiplied her acute cases: patients forgetting their epilepsy meds or their insulin injections; others inadvertently skipping their dialysis appointments, or eating foods to which they are deathly allergic.

Against my better journalistic judgment, I tell her about my investigative reporting piece on the amnesia. She's very interested and asks lots of questions. I swear her to secrecy, then whisper in her ear.

"I think I found a reliable pattern in the onset of amnesia."

"Really?" Her beautiful face lights up with excitement and she begs me to tell her more. I lean over again, inhaling the fresh smell of bergamot on her neck.

"Whatever caused the amnesia started somewhere south first, but I'm not sure how far south." However south it is, I will have to go there, I tell her, hoping I sound like a fearless Clint Eastwood.

"That's fantastic, Max."

In her umber eyes, there's delight, maybe even a hint of admiration. She doesn't seem worried about me at all, but instead, is actually rooting for me. With one enthusiastic smile, she gives me all the confidence I never had.

At dessert, it's Rani's turn to lean over and murmur into my ear.

"Did you go see a therapist?"

I know my drug problem is a deal breaker for a woman with her self-discipline.

"I had my first session," I say. "A shrink who actually knows about war. She said I made huge progress since the amnesia." I don't tell Rani about the notes I'm carrying close to my heart, detailing Josephine's death—or about the relapse and the all-nighter at the ER. What burdens our pasts are, what mountains we drag around every day of our lives. I am tired of hauling things that are heavier than me.

"I'll tell you a secret though, this beautiful hour with you has been a lot more therapeutic," I say, kissing her hand.

Rani doesn't snatch it away this time. She's getting used to a French lover and will never go back.

After dinner, Rani gives me a ride to my place a few blocks away. She parks the car in a dark spot. We can barely see each other. Only our eyes reflect the occasional car passing by. We chat in her car for a little longer, but I decide against asking her up to my studio, which would make all her ethical alarms go off.

The Cabernet is my friend, yielding her lips to mine. Like wine, every kiss has its own personality. Hers is bold, complex, sensual on the tongue, a ripe bouquet of sun-drenched blackberries.

It feels like she's the first woman I touch. Everything

about her is surprisingly soft, her cheeks, her hair, her fuzzy sweater, her hands, which smell of rubbing alcohol and her leather steering wheel.

In the crucible of darkness and warmth that is her car, I carpet her neck with kisses. I know then that her desire for me is no longer a prayer in my imagination, but a real, pulsing thing, as alive and physical as mine. It makes me light-headed. She lets me caress her breasts. They are heavy and perfectly round.

It all feels like the very first time, her breathless kisses, her hands sliding over me. This must be the one gift of the amnesia. In the dark, I hoist her hips over my lap, a preview of what is in store for us next time we find ourselves alone in her apartment. In this instant, I don't care about the wretched past. *We* don't remember anything, but our lips, our limbs know exactly what to do. It's the best of both worlds: experienced bodies and virgin minds.

For a time, we forget the chains of the past, our mortality, and the unnatural days we've endured.

"When can I see you next?" I whisper.

She doesn't answer, but only places her finger on my lips for me to kiss.

When I wave goodbye, I can't remember the last time I felt happier. It's the first joyful memory I've formed since the amnesia. It makes this fresh experience of Rani intoxicating, as there are no other positive memories either to compete with it or to be compared to it.

I walk back up to my studio, and immerse myself in the one good memory I now own, its colors fresh, like today's Polaroid picture. I imagine the texture of Rani's sweater, the shade of her lipstick, the strand of her hair sticking out, which made her look like a woman who'd just made love. I can still hear her laughter, her voice, like music flowing out of her chest. It's the first memory I want to replay. Most of all, I revel in the kisses I managed to extract from her, as though they are gems still rattling in my pocket.

Maybe love is my drug of choice.

I fantasize about making love to Rani, until I naturally fall asleep. For once, my bed feels like a warm, comforting cocoon.

17

_____

Chen

Stealing a clean ID was the easy part. It's slim pickings on the job listings, and the airheads don't even remember the openings they'd posted before their noodles got wiped. I finally find a few museum security guard positions listed— Getty, LACMA, MOCA—but they ask for a resume and references. Now, how is a high-school drop-out like me gonna convince a lah-di-dah museum executive that I'm squeaky-clean, law-abiding, and will protect their stuck-up art like it's my baby sister? Makes you wanna just go out and rob a bank all over again.

I crack open a Johnny Walker to keep me company. What's the point in trying to reason without a buzz? You can do this shit, Chen. You just gotta plan your dance moves ahead of time. That's the difference bro, between a small job and the big time, between the lowly pickpockets who live wallet to wallet—and the smart pros, who score big bank accounts and can afford a lazy retirement for themselves.

Still, it's gonna be tough to wait so long for the prize. Hell, I can get a faster buck begging at the traffic light. Anyways, you'd better get your act together, Chen, if you're going to land a gig at one of them museums. If you wanna pull the wool in front of some big-ass eyes, it's gotta be now or never, just like that memory man said on TV.

On the motel stationery, I scribble what might look good on a hoity toity C fucking V. The Museum of Modern Art in New York is impressive. Military service is a plus. It'd give me some respect, so they don't look at my lean Asian frame and go, "*That* dude's gonna protect my sorry ass?" Security guard at a school proves they trusted me around kids. And security detail for parties shows I have class. Put it all on the East Coast, so the slackers get lazy making long distance calls in a different time zone. Talking to a busy New Yorker with a mean accent is nobody's idea of a good time. Besides, if I worked a museum in N.Y.C., they'd be lucky to have me in L.A.

With this slavin' job hunt, I'm gonna be on the library computer every day. Why make it so hard to earn an honest living, man? Then they wonder why so many decent people are on welfare.

And while I wait, I have to keep my hands under my behind, not get caught doing anything stupid. I peek at the cash stash stitched up inside my jeans. Not bad. Can do. Not like I got rich on anybody's back like those Wall Street boys. I should get myself a suit. Can't show up in sneakers, either, so I'll have to throw in some dress shoes. And a clean haircut. Pricy, pricy being a salaryman. Soon I'll have to dry clean my effing clothes too.

18

Max

Just when I stopped expecting it, Brownell calls me on Skype, a full view of Central Park spread out at his feet like a doormat. I make sure that only I and the wall behind me are on camera. He doesn't need to see that my studio is indistinguishable from a holding cell.

His voice sounds underwater, despite the good connection.

"I commend you for your excellent journalistic instincts seconds after the collective lobotomy," he says.

It's a belated compliment, as my Syria video has been out for over a week. In our industry, it's considered compost by now. I'm sure he's going to ask me to do something unpleasant.

Jeffrey Brownell is one of those suave, well-preserved metrosexuals who can pull off a skinny Yves Saint Laurent suit straight off the runway. He makes aging look like the best phase of life. Something about all his sophisticated props makes you feel small in comparison, like you're still crawling in diapers.

"When are you going back?" he says abruptly.

"To Syria?" I ask, incredulous.

"Yeah, for a follow-up report. The amnesia frenzy is dying down. People are finally interested in where things left off."

"You want me to go to a battlefield and wait around for blood to spill?" I say.

"If you really want to put it that way. Last time I checked, that *was* your job description," he says.

I must be working for an asshole.

"Nothing is going on there right now," I say. "The *Post* beat us to it anyway—and it ended up right before the obits."

"It can all reignite with no warning, you know that," he says.

"They forgot they hated each other. Give them a few months to figure it out again, Jeff."

"Jeffrey," he corrects.

"Actually, I have an investigative piece in mind."

Brownell laughs.

"*Mon cher* Max," he says, flaunting what sound like his only two words of French, "there's a world of a difference between a war correspondent and an investigative reporter."

It's useless arguing with the guy, one of those who prefers to hear himself talk anyway.

"Don't tell me it's about the memory spiel," he says.

I don't correct him.

"Good, because it's no longer selling papers," he says. "Every little nobody fancies himself to be a memory expert right now. It's the new Holy Grail: no one will find it. Don't chase your tail, Max. How about interviewing some Syrian rebels and soldiers, so we're the first there when things start up again?"

That's hardly news, I want to tell him. In reality, there have been no active front lines since the amnesia. War zones are swarming like snake dens, but nobody's biting. It's been enough time for people to rediscover the old list of grievances: lack of food, jobs, equality, freedom. But apparently the blind rage needs more time to build up. Or maybe no one wants to pick a fight with their brain in total eclipse. Frankly, I don't care if it takes them five minutes or six months to figure out that they still know how to work a rocket-propelled grenade—and who deserves one. I want to try something less depressing than watching helplessly while people are exterminated like ants.

"Look, just give me unpaid leave for a month," I say.

Brownell sighs.

"Nope, you're still on payroll—but you've got to tell me what you've been doing with all the data Melinda's been sneaking out to you. She loves you all, but she loves her job even more." Now that he's getting worked up, Brownell sounds like a sea monster calling from the ocean floor. "And bullshit won't cut it this time. Emergency calls on The Day can only mean one thing. It's about the amnesia, isn't it?"

I nod.

"I told you, we can't sell papers with amnesia on every page. We're not a neuropsych textbook. Besides, all the speculation about amnesia is overdone till the sun blows up."

"It's a different angle," I try.

"You know how many times a day I hear 'different angle?' Tell me what you're up to, and I get to tell you where it stands in the universe of angles."

What I've discovered seems petty now, some random noise that I can't even explain with a made-up theory.

"You don't realize there are armies of you spawning the

same exact thoughts because you're all feeding on the same global news dump," he says.

I know this is the disgusting truth. It makes me feel small, fragile, insignificant. Just a piece of trash floating in the great Pacific garbage patch.

"Where *you* shine is on the frontlines. That's where I want you. Melinda will book you in two days," he says, then signs off.

I close my eyes. Why am I still working for this guy? He breaks my balls, pisses me off, and gives me a headache. My muscles are all tensed up, begging for chemical relief. No. Not again. Not after the nice dinner with Rani. I conjure up the soothing memories I have of her, her touch, her scent, her warmth. They are the only luxury I own.

Back on my computer, I consider deleting the data, the maps, the pattern, and the silly hopes that I could contribute anything. My sole value seems to be my ability to risk my own life so that the dead and dying are not forgotten. That's the only thing the world wants of me. This is how a man becomes a pigeon, hiding in the same hole for the rest of his life.

My back-up phone rings. It's such a foreign sound that I don't even know what to do. I fumble with it before finally picking up.

"Listen sweet pea, I ain't booking you on any trip to Syria," says Melinda. "I'm gonna transfer you to Brownell again, and you tell him what you've found exactly. I told you, he's happier when he knows what everybody is up to."

I don't know if her honeysuckle works on Brownell, but he's now on the line.

"Whatever it is, you have three minutes to pitch it," he says. "It's not money until it's out of your head, verified, and copyrighted."

Although he looks like a high-brow, intellectual editor,

Brownell's really a bean counter. He'd be just as successful in the Diamond District or the Mafia.

"Fine. When I mapped the first amnesia-related 911 calls across ten states and Mexico, I found a pattern. The very first calls that day were in Mexico, the Florida Keys, Southern Texas, and Hawaii. The last calls were up in Alaska." I pause for effect, but Brownell isn't impressed.

"Ever heard of time zones?" he says.

"I accounted for time zone—that's not all of it. Time zone simply explains why Western states like Hawaii—where people were still sleeping when the amnesia struck—had fewer bellwether calls." I tell him how the Southernmost areas of Mexico called first, followed by the Southern US States. The Northernmost called last, even though most of the country was awake on a weekday, and perfectly capable of calling 911 at the same time. "What's more important is that on The Day, something was spreading north, Jeffrey—and spreading very fast."

"How fast?"

"Minutes, seconds."

"Too fast to believe," he says. "It could be old clocks that aren't synchronized. The world's clocks aren't all made by Swiss watchmakers, you know."

"Fair enough, but unsynchronized clocks in the US and Mexico would show a random pattern. This is very much systematic," I say. "We need data from something much further South, like Australia, South America."

There's silence on the other end, as Brownell tallies the running cascade of updates he's seen lately, to decide if he's heard anything remotely like it. Brownell can identify the fresh scent of breaking news immediately, because it has the same smell as money.

"We can't be talking about this on the phone. Send me

everything you've got, and get on the next flight. See you tomorrow."

That's the best compliment I'll ever get. It means Brownell knows this is the most concrete lead we have so far.

19

Max

In the gray hours of the morning, I land in New York City, all crumpled by the redeye. Melinda is even taller than I imagined. She tells me that she and Brownell worked through the night, mapping the Australian emergency calls she'd extracted earlier that evening, while the Aussie government workers were still at their desks and disoriented enough to relinquish such things freely to a sweet-talking Southerner who claims to be affiliated with Cornell University. I'm impressed. Brownell's not the type to do any of the digging himself—unless he knows there's gold right underneath his feet.

The dark Southern belle leans down and whispers in my ear.

"Good luck, darlin'."

"I'll need it, darling," I say, startling her.

The *Times* whipmaster glares at his computer, designer vest flung aside, a grin on his face. His office smells less like cologne and more like a men's locker room. Brownell shakes my hand and eyes my tired face.

"Jeez, are they feeding you plankton in California? Melinda, bring this kid something to eat."

Melinda consoles me with coffee and a fat New York bagel with extra cream cheese, while Brownell points to a color-coded map of Australia on his computer screen.

"Look at this beauty," he says.

The first calls came from the southernmost tip of the continent. Same pattern even that far south.

"We need to see Chile and Argentina too," I say.

"South America will be tough. A bunch of countries with no heads or tails," says Brownell. "Every time we beg for something, we leave crumbs behind. Melinda and I will fill in the blanks without handing out hints."

Something definitely started South, but I had no idea we'd have to look as far south as the South Pole.

"I need to go to Antarctica," I say, my eyes still on the screen.

"That's what I was hoping you'd say. Can you take it?" Brownell skims my forearms, as if trying to reassure himself of the presence of at least one percent body fat. He knows I'm the type to find even L.A. winters chilly—that must be why he let me live in the wrong city.

"A bit of wind chill is nothing compared to Syria," I say stoically.

"That's what I like to hear. Look, you're definitely onto something," he says. "We're together on this. I'll stick my neck out for you here, because the frickin' South Pole isn't exactly a cheap destination. It'll deplete my budget and put my job—and yours—on the line if we find a big zero at the end."

"I'll find something. I can smell it from here," I say.

"We'll say you're doing a piece on global warming or snowflakes or some other fuzzy shit of that nature," he says.

"OK."

"Keep a low profile. We need to have something for people to chew on when we break this story. Otherwise, we'll just pave the way for a flock of reporters to go crash the party before we do."

Nice to know he's just as paranoid.

"The Feds must be keeping this to themselves, the bastards—and watching us fill the newspapers with baloney every day. So they're not going to be happy with you there."

"I can do this," I say, trying to convince myself.

20

Chen

The crazies at the Getty actually call me in for an interview. For days, I celebrate with my dwindling personal bar, until I realize I've got homework to do. It's time to camp out at the library computer, and memorize places, dates, names of security directors, and trivia about the gigs I'd slapped on my resume. I come up with minor celebrities who own condos in Manhattan, but who'd be impossible to track down as client references. Turns out growing a scrappy goatee takes more care than an orchid garden. It's a crumb-trap too. But it helps me look the age on Maxi-Million's ID.

When I finally walk through the Getty doors, I'm happy to see that their security people are not any more buff than me. They even have a tiny pregnant Indian lady in uniform who looks like she's gonna give birth any minute. As exhausting as it is to cook up a resume and send all these cutesy emails begging for a job, I'm totally at home at the interview. I'm pretty sure lying to a bigwig's face has never been easier. I go on and on about the big-ass parties I covered; the MoMA job I held; and the United Nations International School stint I did. I just follow the golden rule: When you lie, you'd better make sure it's worth something of real value. The part about military service is hard to imagine. Waking up at dawn, running around in the mud with a backpack in the heat, polishing my shoes, and being celibate—that's just not me. So I talk about how the army wasn't my calling after all, and how I decided to secure people domestically, instead of out in Iraqistan.

I keep a close eye on the white lady interviewing me. She nods her straggly gray head, agreeing that the wars are not her cup of tea either. She's more interested in paintings than people. She just wants to get this part over with, so she can go back to wheeling and dealing in the lofty art world. Her desk has its own skyline of tall, messy piles of papers. I bet she's a hoarder with ten cats at home. She's one sour puss, with so much to figure out before the museum can open its doors again to the public.

"Great, thanks for coming in today," she says abruptly. "We'll check your references and be in touch." She gives me a limp hand to shake, and goes back to worshipping her computer screen.

I don't know what's gonna happen, and I'm not sure if I even made a decent impression. Those references could be a real problem too. The gray lady is the kind of artsy fartsy to be on the phone with New York City every day of her life— no biggy for her. My name could also be a hiccup, if my buddy Maxi-Million survives his chemical stupor and reports his driver's license missing.

I leave her office in a funk, and head to the Getty cafeteria anyways, to have a little bite and get a feel for things while I'm here.

"You're looking smart," says the gal dishing out the meatloaf. She's wearing the L.A. uniform: fake highlights, fake nails, fake boobs.

I smile shyly. I didn't know I look that good in one of them suits. That's one thing a lean Asian has goin' for him: he can tuck his shirt in without extra fat squeezing out at the waistline.

"Cute goatee," says the Mexican chick who's serving up the side dishes.

Women are so easy to please, when it comes right down to it. They make themselves appear so complicated, when they're just as simple as men. It's just that they drool over different things, like a man's shiny shoes, instead of his package.

"So what would you like on the side, honey?" The meatloaf gal bats her five-dollar eyelashes from Walgreens.

Look at that, you wear a new suit and they start callin' you honey. Figures, in this gold digger State.

"Creamed corn and onion rings," I say.

She hands my plate to the Mexican girl, who piles on the onion rings.

"When's the museum going to open?" I ask.

"Dunno," says the blond. "They're still trying to make sure they have all their ducks in a row, like the rest of us."

"It's not like anybody's in the mood for art right now," says the cute Mexican gal.

"Is the staff happy here?" I ask.

"Old Paul Getty left so much money behind that everyone's gotta be happy. Heck, even the customers go in for free," says the blond one.

"Nice to share the bounty with the small people," I say. "You don't hear of nothin' for free no more."

"Nuh-uh," says the Mexican chick.

The onion rings are the best I can remember. This is a good omen. Hopefully I'll get my ass in the door of this Getty Shmetty.

The Getty email in my inbox is from the same gray lady who interviewed me. "Dear Mr. Cattelain," it starts. "We were unable to connect with your references from past positions in New York City at this time. Because of your excellent experience and your flawless background check, we are offering you a position as Security Guard I at our institution. However, this offer remains temporary and retractable for any reason at any time, until we have completed our reference check."

I can't believe my luck. Landing a security job around some of the most expensive artwork in the US of A puts me in a good mood. And a good mood turns me into one horny son of a gun. I weigh the skinny stash of Hamiltons I've got left from the bank. Now that I'll be on Ol' Getty's payroll soon, I can afford a little action—if the ladies didn't forget what they did for a living, that is. I bet I can remember some good moves too.

21

Max

At JFK, my companion for the trip introduces himself as Arnljotur Ulfhrafn Lop, a guest lecturer in Icelandic history who was a one-time contributor to the *Times*. Melinda described him as the only "expert" available immediately—not exactly a stellar recommendation. I explain to him that we need easily pronounceable names on risky missions, preferably no more than two syllables long, hence my own shortened name. He doesn't remember his nickname, so I give him one: Antlop. A native of Iceland, the fellow knows about wind chill, frostbite, and the hundred types of snow. But the more I ask him about our destination, the more I realize he's just as clueless on the opposite side of the planet. It's his first time in Antarctica too.

Antlop doesn't look like the typical Nordic. He has a darker complexion than me, and brown scratchy wiry hair that never stays in place. Because of all his sharp limbs sticking out everywhere, he never properly fits in any chair

—and so is constantly shifting position, crossing and uncrossing his grasshopper legs.

We're only on the first leg of the trip—New York to Santiago—but I can already tell Antlop is going to sap what's left of my sanity. A tireless talker, he can deliver entire lectures about all manner of factoids, even if he can't remember where he was born. He gives me an unsolicited speech about the history of skis. He tells me in great detail about the volcanic eruption of Eyjafjallajökull, which reminded the rest of the world that there is a small country named Iceland. Antlop even catalogues all of the Icelandic culinary specialities that I should try if I ever visit. He swears by his mother-in-law's salted whale, and tells me his boys' favorite treat is fermented shark. None of this makes me want to go there any time soon, lest all Icelandics are this verbose.

"I need a moment of silence," I tell him when we land in Chile.

Antlop feigns incomprehension.

"Please, for the love of God, stop talking—at least until tomorrow," I say.

In reality, this only gets me a ten-minute moratorium. As soon as his indignant look fades, it's quickly replaced by some urgent thought he wants to impart to a man he only met yesterday. There are only three sad solutions to this problem: pack him on the next plane; leave him behind somewhere; or gag him. First, I need to learn a few tricks from the Nordic fellow, then he is history.

As our plane approaches Antarctica, Antlop explains how the land mass we see is really a thick ice sheet, particularly in the South Pole, where we're headed.

"The land itself is buried deep under the ice," he says.

"Is the ice sheet stable for landing?" I ask.

"They use ice-penetrating radar to make sure there are no crevasses on the runway."

"How deep are these crevasses?"

"Theoretically, as deep as the ice sheet," says Antlop. "About a mile deep."

This sends a chill through my bones. He hands me a pill.

"For altitude sickness. This place is almost ten thousand feet above sea level."

The Lockheed LC-130 Skibird projects her skis to land on a snow-packed runway in the middle of snowy nowhere. That's when it hits me that this will be one of my trickiest assignments. At least in Syria, you can hide behind a wall. Here, there is nowhere the deadly cold can't reach you. Smack in the middle of the continent, the South Pole is very flat, very white, and inhumanely cold. The only color comes from the dome of blue sky above. Even the penguins never stray this far inland. Yet, there is a perverse beauty to it all, like a fairytale death wish.

Now I understand why, back in Manhattan, Antlop had emailed me such a long shopping list of specialized, insulated gear from REI, the outdoor megastore which I'd never until then had reason to visit. The mucus in my nose turns into pesky snowflakes, making it impossible to breathe. Even my eyeballs try to see what it's like to freeze. The parka, gloves, boots, goggles, thermals, wind pants, and other 'regulation gear' that Antlop had recommended save my life in the first ten minutes on the continent. I just wish Antlop had also added earplugs to the list of essentials.

Supposedly, it's summer here now. The thought of the sun shining around the clock makes me nervous. It's possible that I won't be able to sleep at all, and that my insomnia will trigger that bad paranoia again. The fact that the sun won't set completely feels like time is going backwards before it goes forwards again. Antlop assures me that the twenty-four-hour sunshine plays in our favor, making it the warmer, glorious season. It's all relative. I can barely tolerate the frigid air piercing through the openings in my ski mask. I want to tell Antlop that the desolate landscape would be more beautiful if it were not accompanied by his constant running commentary.

Melinda instructed us to go to the Amundsen-Scott South Pole Station managed by the National Science Foundation, and explain that we are a "scientific expedition studying whatever Antlop has an expertise in." Brownell recommended that we claim affiliation with his old favorite, Cornell University, rather than with the paper, given that academics usually mind their own microscopic business, compared to big-mouthed reporters like me. With half the *Times* staff impersonating academics from every department over the years, I'm pretty sure that one day Brownell will get sued by his own alma mater.

The airport transport with its gigantic wheels drops us off at the Amundsen-Scott South Pole Station. The reception is cool.

"You're not on the guest list," the polar gatekeeper informs us. Without her XXX-large fleece turtleneck, the pasty lady at the front desk could be sitting at the counter of any DMV in America.

"There must have been a misunderstanding," I say. "Cornell University reserved our spot months ago."

The stout lady emits a fake smile.

"We've turned down folks who reserved their spot *years* ago," she counters. "We're heading into our busy summer season right now. We have senior scientists sleeping on cots in hallways."

"We brought sleeping bags and can easily sleep on the floor," Antlop offers cheerfully.

The polar lady doesn't even respond to that. We came all the way to the South Pole to find just another territorial bureaucrat.

"I wish you had told us before we took our flight," I say.

"I tried, but your Southern belle wouldn't take no for an answer," she says about Melinda. "We can't refuse entry to anybody with a permit, as Antarctica is neutral territory. But if we allowed every scientist who landed to stay at our base, we'd go over capacity in a day. As you can see, even basic resources like food are scarce here."

This is hard to believe, coming from someone who looks like she's never lacked for a calorie. It's a big handicap not to know where we will spend the night. I'm quite sure there's no Hilton on this continent. The rush to get here now seems foolish. I should have planned the trip more carefully.

"Where else can we stay, at least for a couple of nights?" I say.

"There's a Russian base nearby," she says in a snarky tone. "Though they aren't usually welcoming to US citizens. The only other viable option is McMurdo station on the coast. They have more space, but they do have rules and requirements."

"Can you call them for us?"

"Satellites only work two hours a day here," she says.

"I have a satellite phone." I bring out the big bag I've been lugging around and place it on the counter.

She glances at the logo on the case, and informs me that the satellite phone Melinda had procured for me is one of the brands that doesn't work in the South Pole. Great.

"When can you call them then?" I ask.

"In five hours."

"Forget it. We'll fly there," I say.

The fleece lady informs us that there are no flights scheduled between the stations at present.

Antlop and I look at each other. Maybe our best solution is to head back home. Then what? Leave the story to another journalist who made better sleeping arrangements?

"I might have a solution for you," offers the bureaucrat. "We've got a McMurdo vehicle that's been sitting here for quite a while. It needs to be returned to them. If you have clean driving records, good credit, and agree to be financially responsible for the vehicle in transit, we can let you drive it back to them. They'll be grateful for the favor, and will surely let you stay there for a few nights."

"Drive? In the snow?" I mutter. It doesn't seem to be much of a solution to me, but Antlop nods eagerly.

"I can drive in the snow," he says.

"This is Antarctica," I point out.

"Snow is the same everywhere," says Antlop, amused at my ignorance.

She asks for our driver's licenses. Antlop offers his.

"Sorry, I didn't think I'd be renting a car on Antarctica." I give her my passport instead. I don't tell her that I lost my driver's license while shooting up in an alley, and that I didn't exactly have time to go to the actual DMV.

She manages to find my driving record using my license number. Then she asks for my social security number, and runs a credit check, since I'm the one paying.

"So you're employed by the Getty?" she asks, looking at her screen.

This is news to me. Makes no sense, but it's better that these guys think I work at a museum than a newspaper.

"Yeah," I say. "Getty Research Division."

"Does the vehicle have navigation?" Antlop asks her.

"Just follow the McMurdo-South Pole highway, and you won't get lost," says the gatekeeper lady, her smile suspect.

Who knew there is a highway in the middle of nowhere? Then, as an unexpected random act of kindness, the fleece lady fetches us some hot tea and four sandwiches from the cafeteria. She refuses payment for the food, which can only be a bad sign. No one ever asks you to pay for your last meal.

At the underground vehicle depot, an old attendant leads us to what looks like a black tank. The modified Toyota Hilux is set high on four studded wheels that each have the width of four regular tires. Antlop's eyes glint at the sight of all this machine power. With arthritic hands, the attendant attaches a trailer to the back, with its own set of oversized wheels. It's unclear to me why we'd want to haul a trailer, until I see the old man ease six barrels of Jet 1A fuel onto it with a fork lift. Right, there are no gas stations on the ice sheet.

"Do we really need this much fuel?" I ask.

"Whatever you don't use will be refunded when you get there," he tells us. "Better to have more than you need, son."

"I'm not so sure about this," I whisper to Antlop. I turn to the depot guy, "Say, do you know when the next flight is out of here?"

"Not for five days," he says.

"Don't worry, we'll be fine," says Antlop.

The old man shows Antlop how to change the fuel tanks when the time comes. When he asks me to sign off, I almost faint at the price tag: at thirteen thousand a barrel, the total for the fuel alone comes out to seventy-eight thousand dollars. Of course, I also have to agree to replace the custom, fully-loaded truck if something happens to it on the way there. This is what Brownell meant when he said Antarctica wasn't a cheap destination.

Antlop climbs into the shiny new toy first, happy as can be. As soon as I take off my ski mask and goggles inside the freezing vehicle, my stubble clots with frosty flakes crystallized from my breath. This cold doesn't waste any time.

"You know how to build an igloo, just in case?" I ask him.

"Setting up emergency shelter is the first thing you learn in survival training in Iceland," he assures me.

"And you do remember your training?"

"Of course, I had to do this many times. And I have a tent too." Maybe Antlop isn't so clueless, after all.

The "highway" doesn't even qualify as a dirt road. We have to drive around in circles before we locate the head of the compacted snow trail. It's delineated from the rest of the indecipherable snow by minuscule red flags on either side, many of which got knocked out by the wind. It'll be a challenge just to stay on the road.

22

Max

Two hours into it, we see only whiteness behind us and whiteness in front of us. It makes me claustrophobic, despite the openness all around me. It's a true no man's land —and we are not even equipped with a working satellite phone in case of an emergency.

"How far is this place then?" I ask.

"About nine hundred miles," says Antlop.

That explains why we're hauling fuel for a tribe. Here I was thinking it was a three-hour jaunt, at most. I shake my head in disgust for having accepted the DMV lady's poisoned apple.

"At least we have a vehicle," says Antlop to try to cheer me up. "Early explorers did this in skis and sleds."

Right, like I would ever compare myself to such crazy people. Who knew the road to hell was paved with ice? Why I came to this frozen-over hell is a mystery. There's obviously nothing worth reporting on here. Just lots and lots of age-old snow. Brownell will have a heart attack when he sees that he wasted his remaining budget for nothing. On the highway in the middle of nowhere, I expend as many calories swearing as I do maintaining my body temperature.

To Antlop's credit, he manages to ignore my ill humor. The Icelandic is in his element driving the clunky vehicle in the snow, though he's not as good at it as he claims. Fortunately, the chances of colliding into a vehicle or a pedestrian here are nil. When Antlop doesn't talk, he whistles. I stop myself from outlawing whistling in the cabin when I realize it's easier on the nerves than the never-ending chatter. If I just close my eyes and pretend to sleep, it keeps Antlop slightly less chatty.

~

"You should take over," says Antlop.

I must have fallen asleep. I wake up groggy, with a sprawling headache.

"Drive? Me? I've never driven in the snow."

"Practice while I'm still awake," he says. "Go slow and stick to the road. We don't have enough fuel to get lost."

"Are we getting close?"

"Nowhere close. I've been driving for five hours now."

It's hard to believe we've been out here that long already. This at least relieves my anxiety about insomnia. With the 24-hour daylight and the flat, monotonous white terrain, everything looks and feels like everything else, including being awake and asleep.

"Plus, we need to change the fuel tank," says Antlop, starting the long process of donning the layers.

The tank feels heavier than both of us, and not as easy to attach as the attendant made it out to be. The cold is especially harsh when your body is sleepy, jetlagged, oxygen-hungry, and has been sitting in a steaming car all day. We may as well be on the moon out here.

Reluctantly, I slide into the driver's seat and grasp the oversized steering wheel. Antlop hops into the back seat and soon I hear him peeing in an empty plastic bottle. No one wants to risk losing any key body parts to frostbite. He serves me the remainder of the tea—now so cold it qualifies as iced—and we eat the last of the sandwiches.

"We didn't bring much food," I say.

"I brought some protein bars with me. We can each have two or three for the rest of the trip—and we can melt fresh snow to drink."

It's tempting to tell him what I really think of protein bars, but they're better than breaking down muscle.

Driving on the snow is not as hard as I thought. My main preoccupation is avoiding speed, as you lose control of the truck in seconds. The tiny red flags on the road are few and far between, some of them flung far away by the unrestrained wind. Otherwise, to be fair, the road has fewer potholes than New York or L.A. I try to relish the forced road trip. It is beautiful here in its own wicked way. We pass by curvaceous, gigantic dune-like formations of snow, which Antlop called sastrugi. They remind me of fresh whipping cream. I use this time to myself to daydream of Rani. I hope she doesn't think I'm making excuses after I had left a voicemail telling her I was going on a long assignment. I wonder if she's thinking of me.

Antlop turns out to be as noisy asleep as he is awake. The fellow not only snores like an animal, but occasionally talks in his sleep, in jagged Icelandic utterances. I long for earplugs like nothing else in this world.

While Antlop is snoozing, amorphous clouds slowly displace the stark blue. Initially, I welcome the reduced glare from the sun reflecting wildly on the ice. But hours later, the sky and the ice fuse together, so I can't tell anymore where the land begins and ends. It feels like we're driving through a cloud. Maybe it is a low hanging cloud. It occurs to me that I haven't seen a red flag in a while. Why are they so stingy with them?

It feels like I'm turning in circles. I've already used up most of the tank. I slow down a bit, and while I'm still fumbling with the GPS to make sure I'm still on course, one of the rear tires hits something. The truck stops. My first thought is something hard, like a boulder. Something tells me there are no boulders here.

When I press harder on the accelerator, the vehicle lurches and refuses to move forward. With more gas, the tires squeal, but the vehicle doesn't budge. Then the engine chokes and comes to a halt.

The ignition doesn't respond. Damn it. I'm still trying to figure out what to do, when the vehicle sinks back in one jolt. The sound of a muffled crack. Shit. A crevasse. If it cracks wide open, the vehicle will drop all the way down the ice sheet. I shout to Antlop, but he doesn't wake up. I scoot out of the truck, but I don't dare run, in case the ice is unstable. I could be standing on a mere snow bridge that's hiding a crack. I walk away as gingerly as I can, then yell to Antlop again. The guy's sleep is like a coma. Even with my coat on, the cold outside hits me. It's probably minus forty—but without all the extra gear, it feels like minus infinity.

I'm slowly freezing, while Antlop is asleep in a vehicle that's about to fall through the ice sheet. From this angle, it's clear the rear tire is well jammed in a crevasse. I shove my fingers into my pockets, but they're already goners. Another muffled break follows, and the vehicle drops further into the widening crack. Shit. I yell Antlop's name again at the top of my lungs.

Antlop finally wakes up, in a foul mood. The first thing

he notices is that the vehicle is stationary and that I'm not in the driver's seat.

"Are you fucking mad turning the engine off? It can freeze up and never turn on again," he says.

"I didn't turn it off," I say calmly.

"You left it in gear?" he snaps.

I watch in horror as Antlop jumps from the backseat into the driver's seat with a thud, and grabs for the ignition. It doesn't obey, neither the first time nor the second time around.

"Damn it!" says Antlop, slamming the steering wheel with both hands. "A dead engine is our death out here."

He tries the ignition again. Again it screeches, but doesn't catch.

By the violence of his movements, it's clear that he hasn't registered the problem yet. He's so distraught by the engine that he hasn't realized the vehicle is canted slightly backwards.

"We hit a crevasse," I tell him as calmly as possible.

He finally understands why the vehicle is tipped back at an angle, and why I'm not in it. He stops talking or swearing. The snow stifles all noise, including that of the wind. So when we hear the sickening sound of a coconut shell splitting, we know it's the crevasse deepening further. In Antlop's eyes, there's a sudden realization that the Toyota will be swallowed into the fissure any moment—with him in it.

23

Chen

The first day on the job, I'm assigned a buddy guard, who's supposedly there to train me—but I bet he's keeping an eye on me too. Mielek has a thick Eastern European accent and skin so pale you can see a 3-D web of blue veins right through it. That's just too white, man. He has permanent bags under his eyes, and a steely look that gives patrons the chills. Mielek aspires to be a statue in the next life. He doesn't even speak when spoken to. It makes you feel needy for wanting to say hello to another human being—and outright desperate for wanting to talk about the weather.

But the guy is no zombie. The fact is, Mielek is a walking video-camera: nothing escapes him. He'll know by the end of the day that the new Asian hire has never been a security guard an hour in his life. A second day of this torture and Mielek will know that I really belong on the other side of the bars, so to speak. After all that hard work, I'm gonna get booted out in no time.

I give myself a good talking to in the men's room. Come on, Chen, being a professional means you gotta save your despair for after business hours. I try to act like the security guards in the movies I studied. Gotta just focus on the patrons, because that's what security guards do. Later on, if I'm still here—and far from Mielek's human microscope—I can afford to look at the artwork more closely. I'm all nerves around him, but I still try to look bored most of the time, since the boredom of security guards is legend.

I must've really overdone the yawning and can't-give-a-damn look, as the first thing Mielek says when he finally breaks his vow of silence in the cafeteria is, "You don't really care about art, do you?"

"I've seen more art in my lifetime than I really want," I say about my nonexistent N.Y.C. experience. "If you ask me, only the nude women are worth the paint. The rest is shit."

The earful satisfies Mielek. He goes back to eating his tuna salad sandwich and recording every facial twitch I make. I'd better remember to show more interest in the nudes when we're back in the galleries.

"Why d'you have a French name?" he asks.

I had no idea my buddy Maxi-Million's name is French. That explains why nobody knows how to pronounce it, starting with me.

"I've got a little French in me, that's why," I say. Somewhere in my brain I seem to know that those frog legs colonized the place, like everyone else and their cousin in Europe, and that's why you can find French baguettes all the way in Vietnam.

Mielek smirks and decides to call me Frenchie. I don't fight it. I figure it's better to have the nickname of a poodle than the name of a dead man.

One good thing happens to me that day: that friendly

Mexican cafeteria girl gives me an extra helping of onion rings to welcome me to the museum.

At least Mielek uses the rest of his lunch hour to chain-smoke out in the back instead of squeezing me about past jobs. That Communist son of a gun is bound to see right through my lies too. I bet in Mielek's shady past, he'd been posted at one of those military checkpoints, where he decided if a carload of people was allowed to escape or die.

Back at the galleries, I sit down to rest my legs a bit, maybe rest my eyes a little too after waking up so early.

Next thing I know, Mielek is poking my chest with a sturdy index finger. I completely freak out. I let out a scream, but he slams his hand on my mouth so what comes out sounds like a hamster squealing in a plastic bag.

"No sleeping on payroll," Mielek whispers in my ear, before taking his smelly tuna salad fingers off me.

I didn't even realize I'd dozed off on the chair. One more wink and I'll be fired. I'd better set a proper bedtime if I want to survive this fucking boot camp.

"I need stronger stuff than the pot of boiled socks that passes for coffee around here," I say.

Mielek nods in agreement. He doesn't know that I only drink coffee when there's no beer.

I start roaming around and find some nudes to look at. Blubbery bottoms and droopy breasts that look filled with lead pellets. Beats me why a self-respecting artist would paint naked middle-aged women who look better clothed. I look away. Daydreams of dainty Thai chicks in lingerie and revealing sarongs come to my rescue. That's when I come across a still life with two pomegranates and a teacup. Someone put it in a gaudy golden frame to give ignorant patrons the hint that it's important. My eyes lock on the name of the painter. Even I know Cézanne—he must be famous. There are so many dollar signs crowding my thoughts that I bump into one of those old bags who dress to the nines, bring out their smelly mink coats, and smear on their tackiest lipstick just for the dead white men staring back at them from picture frames.

"Watch your step, mister," she grumbles. She wags a scary finger with a giant ruby ring that'll never come off.

I slink back in the corner to become part of the upholstery again. When I look up, I see that Mielek registered all of it. Shit. This can only mean one thing: bye bye Bangkok.

24

Max

"Don't you want to come out and see?" I keep my voice even, and try to convince Antlop to just get the hell out of the vehicle. The ice can easily split fast on either side of the crevasse—I'm not far enough myself.

"Don't tell me anything," he says.

His face turns gray, as the reality of it all sinks in. It's the first time that the fellow remains perfectly quiet. It's better that he comes out of the Toyota slowly anyway, so I back off.

Standing outside, even with my coat on, I feel the full force of the cold now. It hurts, menacing from the surface of my skin and from the inside of my bones. Without the rest of the gear, my exposed face and gloveless hands turn numb in minutes. There's no way we can survive here for long without the vehicle or some kind of shelter. If Antlop could in fact build an igloo of sorts, would it keep us warm until a search party finds us? The problem is that no one will even know we're missing—except the bureaucrat at Amundsen. Like she even remembers us.

Instead of abandoning the truck, Antlop pulls the key out of the ignition and inspects it. He blows on it for a while, warming it with his breath, as if to melt an invisible layer of ice on it. Superstitious behavior. He starts fiddling with the ignition. We're about to die because of my stupidity.

In the absolute quiet, another tearing sound startles us. The Toyota lurches back again, slamming Antlop's head against the head rest. He rattles off some long Icelandic swearword.

"Just get out of there, Antlop," I shout.

"No." He closes his eyes, immobile, unwilling to shift his weight around in the driver's seat.

I don't want to see this, and turn away to face the horizon, which is still clouded over by a fine icy mist. The fairy-tale snow around me is all white and innocent—even if it can eat people whole.

Antlop is picking at the ignition again, making a screeching noise.

Then the unexpected sound: the engine coughs, gurgles, sputters, then against all odds, begins to hum.

It's hard to believe he did it. Antlop's eyes are still closed. He's listening to the engine like it's a song. Then, as if he has all the time in the world, he puts on his gloves and ski mask. With the engine running, he steps out of the vehicle and finally inspects the crevasse.

It's an ugly sight. The right rear tire is jammed into a clean crack in the ice. On the inside, the fissure has a ghostly blue hue. I can't get myself to look any deeper. I don't know if I'd see the black ocean all the way at the bottom—or some underground river flowing over the bedrock. On the other side of the crevasse is the trailer. If it widens suddenly, we'll slip into it in no time. Walking slowly, Antlop takes a wide berth around the thinner part of the crevasse. He gently disengages the fuel trailer on the other side and orders me to clear out, as far away from the crack as possible. I oblige.

Antlop actually has the guts to get back into the driver's seat after what he saw. With a lighter vehicle, he manages to ease the rear tire out of the hole. I stand there in the cold, watching Antlop drive away. The Toyota trundles far into the distance, until it looks like an insect in the fog. What the hell? Antlop doesn't have to go that far to make a safe U-turn. He's punishing me for leaving the engine in gear, for straying off the nebulous road. I just stand there, with some seventy grand of fuel keeping me company, until the truck is a speck of dirt.

I feel curiously calm. I'm not about to start running, if that's what Antlop wants me to do. My knee won't do it anyway; chilled, it feels like it'll snap out of its socket. Turns out the cold doesn't just numb your fingers and joints, but your mind too. Truth is, I'm more fed up with life than he can imagine. Fuck it. He doesn't realize that I'm more willing to dive into the crevasse than beg him to save me.

My only regret is that I won't have made love to Rani before I die. We could have had a great night together, if it weren't for the stupid rules women carry around like corsets.

Oh, well, if I'm going to freeze out here, I may as well have a cigarette. With ghostly white fingers, I extract the pack from my breast pocket. The cigarette is cold and brittle, like it was left in the freezer. I light her up, and take that wicked first draw that damns all smokers. Despite my dead fingers, and my clacking lips, it's the best smoke of my life, a small consolation.

Through the whiteness around me, the black stain of the truck reappears in my field of vision. Antlop has decided to come back. Maybe the prospect of a manslaughter charge spooks him. More likely, he knows he needs the extra fuel. The Icelandic makes a wide circle around the fissure, driving extra slowly, then backs up on the other side of it. In silence, without looking at me or the crack, he rotates the trailer hook, and attaches it to the truck. He drives farther away from the crevasse and waits, the vehicle stationary, the engine running, which I understand to be a begrudging invitation to join him. I walk up to the truck slowly, not sure if he's teasing me.

Antlop and I are barely on speaking terms when we change the fuel tank again. The hunger and caffeine withdrawal gnaw at what little is left of our patience. Before we get back in the vehicle, I notice the snow on the ground is uneven and striated, but I don't know what to make of it.

"What's this?" I show him the bumpy snow under our feet.

"We're on a glacier. You bumbled off road, hit a crevasse, and wasted a tank of fuel—but at least you found the fucking glacier," says Antlop.

"We're supposed to be on a glacier?" This is very unsettling.

"It's the only way through," he says.

It's tempting to ask, then I decide it's better not to know whether glaciers are scarred with crevasses. Ignorance is sometimes good for you.

Once inside, I curl myself into the heated passenger seat, trying to regain lost body heat, knowing Antlop won't let me drive again. He's giving me the cold shoulder, ignoring me completely. Antlop brought back fresh snow in a Ziploc bag and placed it near the heat vent. We wait till it melts, then take turns drinking from it. The snowflakes taste purer than Evian water—probably because they've never once touched the earth. Afterwards, Antlop dips a t-shirt in the remaining ice water and wipes his face. I pass on the symbolic hygiene. Surely the cold has sterilized the entire surface of my body by now.

When we finally locate the joke of a 'highway' once more, Antlop decides to talk to me again. I knew he couldn't keep quiet for long.

"So why are we here?" he asks. "Is it really to study snowflakes?"

I want to tell him that we're looking for something far more elusive. Brownell and I can't risk a leak at this stage, so I just give him something vague but true.

"You never know where the news will be tomorrow," I say.

"Well, it's not here. Look around, you see any news 'fit to print?'" he scoffs, unnecessarily loud.

All his fear is coming out as anger now.

"The news—the truth—is here somewhere," I say softly. "We're just not ready to see it, to grasp it. It's still a ruby buried deep underground."

"Rubbish. You just don't trust me."

I don't deny this. He forgets there's a satellite phone in this vehicle—if it ever works—a way for him to relay whatever I tell him to the outside world.

"Whatever, I guess Brownell paid me an extra grand to not ask questions," says Antlop.

"Then don't forfeit it."

"Fuck you," he says. "We almost died out there."

"I know. You saved my life," I say, serious. "Thank you."

He says nothing more for a while.

I'm still too cold and crabby to sleep while Antlop drives over a bumpier terrain now. I'm craving something. What is there not to crave? Warmth, food, coffee, a bed, sex. Maybe even heroin. That too. I should have brought along a little baggie of my own magic 'snow'—just for a day like this, when you don't even know if you're going to live or die.

I'm still taking Rani's meds, mostly because it's my only hope of ever sleeping with her—but they are blah compared to the real thing. Sadly, I can't even remember the last time I had sex, because it was before the amnesia.

Aside from that, there's something else I'm hankering for. There's no news here—not just the kind to write about, but also the kind to read. I remember the old papers I'd hoarded, starting at the Antakya airport. Every time I'd bought a physical paper somewhere, I'd add it to the small pile at the bottom of my backpack, just in case the amnesia strikes back. The newsprint I dig out is stale, crumpled, stained, but legible. There are a few Op-Eds about memory I haven't read yet, written by philosophers, poets, fools struck with five minutes of inspiration. I smile, inadvertently stretching the painfully dry skin on my face. A think piece about war catches my eye, about whether the wars will restart again after The Day.

I throw myself into the comfort of the black and white print, where letters have clear borders, where sentences have a beginning, an end, and preferably a meaning too.

"...We lost more than our childhoods and cherished memories on The Day. We have also been stripped of our cultural, religious, and political differences. Even soldiers can no longer distinguish their enemies from their friends. Will this bring us closer together? Or will our wars resume —simply because they are habitual?

"The amnesia has taken away our old grievances, our cynicism, leaving us like children who have never been hurt. For a short while, we will be idealistic again—before we relearn pain and loss.

"If the Day of Forgetting is to be worth something at all for our trouble, we will have to accomplish something together, all at once, between our first tear and our first shrug. We will have to do something now, during this tender age, during this, our second childhood."

The paper in between my hands, stiffened by the cold, soothes me. Reading, I'm oblivious to the expanse of nothingness behind me and in front of me. For one moment, I forget that we're driving over a glacier that can break again at any moment and engulf us.

Setting the old paper down, I pick up another one from the scrappy pile. That's when I see it, lodged in between the old newsprint, the sealed envelope containing my therapy notes.

Since we landed here, I had completely forgotten about them. I press down on the tape that's not holding up too well in the cold. Antlop glances my way.

"What's that?" he says.

"Nothing." I put the manila envelope back where I found it in the backpack, and gaze at the brightness outside, fighting the urge to sleep.

Look how I almost died without bothering to find out what happened to my dear Josephine. What kind of reporter am I that I deliberately avoid the truth about my own life? I'm so weak. Remembering the dead is the least the living can do. This is the only record of what she had meant to me and how she died—and here I am willing to go into a battlefield, but incapable of opening an envelope.

If I read my past, will I die of grief? Or will it feel like someone else's tragedy? My kneecap was mysteriously fractured by a blunt object four to six months ago—around the same time Josephine died. It makes me wonder if I had been there, if I had witnessed her death, if I had tried in vain to save her. Maybe that is why Sylvia said I was punishing myself.

If I don't remember Josephine, if I don't recognize her

picture, can I still love her? Without my past, what is left of who I am? Am I still the sum of where and how I was raised; of what I've learned and accomplished? Or am I now just walking DNA?

It saddens me that I have been robbed of all my joys, my loves, my Josephine. But I have also been freed from all my disappointments, my sins, my wounds. Our memories may as well have been etched in ice. Ice that has now melted.

And what about the war within, will *it* resume? If our past weighs us down, does forgetting it free us? Or maybe losing our memories just makes us more vulnerable to making the same old mistakes twice. Will I recklessly jump back into a war zone, then drug myself to death?

I look up. The wind has picked up, swirling new snow with old, whiting everything out. My mind too has become a flat, white world, a blank slate, a virgin continent. And so has everyone else's.

I need to keep it this way, for now—if only to have the strength to find out why the amnesia began here, in Antarctica—before it's my turn to become a footnote, a line written in the snow.

25

Chen

After the first week on the job, I'm just beat. They're getting their money's worth out of me, that's for sure. I start bringing Dunkin' Donuts coffee in a thermos just to stay awake, and hand a cup to Mielek to make nice. After he downs the coffee, his face is locked in such terrible pain that I wonder if I should grab the defibrillator. Then I realize it's just Mielek's disturbing smile. Being the coffee guy seems to bring Mielek to my side. That can be handy, especially as my ass is still on the line until they figure out what to do with those made-up references. Once or twice Mielek brings some of his homemade, greasy, impossible-to-digest Eastern European sausage to share with me—and won't take 'no' for an answer. That's as friendly as he gets. In the long lunch hours, I teach him poker. He has so much potential with his natural poker face. But the guy is a sore loser, and will twist your arm till you give him his money back.

Soon enough, I meet the other guards on our floor.

There's Dieguito, a well-groomed Mexican dude who always smells of shaving cream. I catch him in the men's room after lunch one day, shaving the stubble that sprouted between nine a.m. and noon. Then there's Gumphrey, an African-American sister with buttocks that stand as high as my shoulders.

There's really only one perk that comes with this job: this place has a lot of new chicks comin' and goin' every day. They come in here with their dainty toe rings, high-heeled flip-flops, breezy see-through tops that tease and confuse the eye, and pants so tight they may as well have been left at home. It's L.A., after all, the land where wannabes become the real thing. Helps a man beat the boredom anyway.

With so little foot traffic that afternoon, I decide to pace a bit wider than usual, to catch a few glimpses of the Cézanne, maybe check out its camera set-up and the emergency exits nearby. Not that it's a particularly impressive piece—just another pound of fruit by another bored painter. It's famous though *and* it fits in a backpack.

I give out a big, fake yawn as I face the ceiling, looking for the tiny eyes of the cameras. Out of the blue, a police siren explodes in the distance. It drifts closer and closer every second. The wretched noise is like nails on my eardrum. I'm frantically trying to decide what to do, where to go, before I realize I didn't do nothin' illegal yet. Or did I? What about stealing some poor soul's identity? What if the gray lady tried to contact my references and found out I'm lying? And oops, I almost forgot the little bank robbery.

The sirens fill the air now—then stop abruptly. That means only one thing: the cops are on the premises. I stare at the emergency exits—but if I try to scoot, the alarms will trigger like nobody's business. I have nowhere to go. End game.

Act cool, Chen, like a puny security guard on alert, just in case you can still wrangle yourself out of this one. I start pacing again, trying to stamp out the nerves. Soon, I hear hurried footsteps in the staircases. A side door bursts open, and a cop storms out, his hand on his holster, giving me a full-blown panic attack. My bad memories of the slammer may have been wiped clean, but my flight instincts are alive and well. I feel real faint. I need to sit down for a second, catch my breath, get a hold of myself. When I look back to find a chair, I see Mielek sitting on it, smiling, entertained by the show.

"It's just a drill," he says, amused. "They do it every month. That's why we closed an hour early."

26

Max

When I open my eyes, I'm disoriented, unsure where I'd fallen asleep. My head is cold from leaning on the window-pane. My hands are numb, my stomach is cramping with hunger, my muscles aching, because it's time for my Rani pill. The blinding whiteness all around reminds me that I'm in a truck with a stranger, crossing the white continent. Then I notice the mountain range outside my window. Beautiful brown peaks sticking out, like the Alps had been snowed in except for their tops. The snow drift has quietened down, and it's clear and crisp now. Through the windshield straight ahead, I see another mountain range on the other side. The map on the GPS tells me we're on the Beardmore glacier, which carves out an outrageously wide river of snow in between two mountain ranges, the Queen Alexandra and the Commonwealth. It's reassuring to see solid rock.

I hear paper crinkling, and turn to find Antlop in the

driver's seat, the manila envelope clutched in his hand, propped against the steering wheel. He's reading my therapy notes.

"*Bon sang de merde!* What do you think you're doing?"

Rage gushes out of my dry, painful throat. I snatch the notes from his hands, almost ripping them.

"I thought it was about our secret mission here," says Antlop, sheepish.

"It says confidential—or are you fucking blind?"

I don't ever remember feeling this primal anger. It's like a bad chemical has been injected into me. Before I know how to reign it in, how to bring myself down, a physical, violent urge takes over. I punch the bastard full on in the face—for all the shit of this world, for whatever horror took my Josephine away.

Antlop emits a scream, then holds his nose with both hands. Soon, blood seeps through the cracks in his fingers.

I close my eyes in shame. Of course, it didn't resolve anything. But I don't feel like apologizing. The paper in my trembling hands is brittle in the cold. Sylvia's handwriting looks like an ant had pulled itself out of an inkwell and made its way back home blind. My past is encapsulated in just four little pages. Without trying, my eyes latch onto a sentence: "She was a journalist for the *L.A. Times*."

I wince, my mind adding this fact to the mysterious equation that is her death. It already assumes no grave and no ashes, and now the result is even more negative.

It takes everything I have not to read more. My eyes fill with tears, thankfully blurring Sylvia's tiny cursive.

"I shouldn't have. I'm sorry," says Antlop. "And my condolences for your—"

"Don't say another word. Don't go there. I don't want to talk about it—at all or ever. You understand me?"

"I understand," says Antlop, his hands a mess now that the blood has congealed in the cold.

I hand him the wet t-shirt that he'd used to wipe his face. The blood has already dropped on his coat, his pants, the seat of the car. Blood is merciless. It finds its way everywhere, and stays there forever, an indelible reminder of human stupidity, cruelty, and guilt.

"I didn't mean to pry into your private life," says Antlop, trying to keep his tone civilized, only because whatever he's read about me is making him feel sorry for me. "We almost died back there. All I wanted to know is for what exactly."

I suppose a man has a right to know.

"I wish I knew, but I don't," I say, trying to regain my calm. "We came here to follow a lead. That's how it works. It's like hunting without knowing what you might catch. Something moves in the bushes. You smell something. But you don't know the facts until you seize them in your hands.

"I'm not going to lie to you. It could end up being something trivial. It could be nothing at all. Or it could be everything everybody has been waiting for."

He takes this in.

"What we call news is just a truth that we deem important enough to be written up, printed, disseminated, read, and kept forever in the imperfect vault that is the newspaper."

"What's the lead?" he asks, relentless.

"I worked my tail off for that lead," I say. "I can't just give it to you to make you feel better. I know you saved my life, but I just don't give anybody my leads—except my boss, because he can fire me. It took everything I have to be the first reporter to get to this fucking continent at this point in time. I need to keep it that way till my work's done."

"So I'm risking my life for something that you don't feel I deserve to know? Something that may not even be a worthy cause," he says, through a nasal voice and a red-soaked t-shirt.

The truck now has the ugly smell of blood, and it's making me feel sick. I open the window halfway. He doesn't object, even if it'll refrigerate the place. The wind whistles in and dances around like a mean-spirited genie. But at least it neutralizes the stench of men with the smell of snow. It reminds me that there's an ethereal realm, something greater than the dense organic matter we're made of.

It occurs to me that I misjudged Antlop. Perhaps he's not afraid of death, as much as dying for a stupid reason. He's in need of a pep talk.

"We're risking our lives for the truth," I say. "The truth is a worthy cause. Lots of people have died for it." I wonder if Josephine died for the truth, but I try not to dwell on that. "It's not great, but I can think of worse reasons to die."

"I have two sons, you know, and a wife with a psychological problem," he says.

There's fragility in Antlop's sleepless eyes. I look away.

"We're not dying just yet," I say calmly. He might have read something in my notes that's bothering him. I try to remember what unappealing crumbs Sylvia had dropped about my pre-amnesia state of mind. "I didn't come here on a suicide mission, if that's what you're worried about," I say. "I came here to get to the bottom of something important, something your sons and wife would be proud of—if we have the balls to find it."

We eat our last installment of protein bars, washed down with melted snow. Antlop eventually gives in to his fatigue and allows me back behind the wheel. We take turns driving and sleeping, trying not to accuse each other of incompetence during the short periods when we're both awake.

27

Max

Finally, something crops up on the drifting white horizon: the stately Observation Hill—Ob Hill—overlooking McMurdo base. Initially a gray blotch, the base enlarges into a massive compound painted in Lego-block colors. Towering hills of snow have cozied up to the North-facing walls, sealing their tiny windows. In the distance, is a sea of white, with snowy islands far out. It's the Ross Ice Shelf. Unlike the icy desert inland, at least the invisible sea underneath bears life: fish, penguins, and whales. The temperature is more humane here too.

It's nice to drive on real land now, even if it's slush and dark volcanic soil splattered together with slicks of black ice. The research compound looks sleepy. I wonder if it's nighttime? It's hard to keep track after driving nonstop in continuous daylight. They say there's a coffeeshop, and even a bar in Mactown. I'd rather have a full stomach and a cup of coffee before negotiating with McMurdo's resident bureaucrat. But nothing looks open for business. We decide to report to the biggest building.

We have to swerve around several vehicles that have been carelessly parked around the structure. I expected more order here, in a facility run by the US Navy. I unfold my body out of the truck and walk around, happy to be on solid land again. The warmer coastal air is so much gentler on the nostrils too. It's still well below freezing, but not instant frostbite weather. We trek around the enormous structure before locating what looks like the main entrance. It's locked solid.

"Isn't it the busy summer season?" I say, sarcastic.

"Unless the staff was called back home after the amnesia," says Antlop.

That possibility hadn't even crossed my mind till now. That incompetent at Amundsen sent us here on a fool's errand, without even making contact with these guys.

"If the McMurdo folks were called back, you'd think the Amundsen people would have gone home too."

"You'd think," says Antlop. "But the South Pole station is run by the NSF, so maybe it's a different protocol."

We make the rounds of the building again, this time looking up at the windows above for any signs of life. With the glass reflecting the sun's glare, it's hard to tell if there are any lights on inside. I don't see any smoke exhaust from the building heater. The whole place has the secretive silence of cemeteries.

We walk over to a smaller, adjacent building. Not much luck opening these doors either. Another skinny structure nearby also looks abandoned, bolted shut. The place is dead. We both start to fret.

It's time to try the satellite phone again. It beeps on, but fails to work so close to the pole. Useless junk.

Spent from the calorie deficit, now we're worried about

securing shelter. We can easily die of hypothermia out here, despite the warmer temperatures. With only one full barrel of fuel left in our trailer, we don't have enough to drive back to the South Pole Station or any other base—even if we wanted to.

"Let's drive around," I say. "Maybe we'll see some sign of life."

We get back in the truck.

McMurdo looks like an abandoned auto-assembly town in the Midwest. It has an industrial feel, and of course, there's not a single tree. It's all the more depressing without any people.

Driving toward the iced up coast, I'm hoping to spot some seal or penguin popping out of a hole in the ice, just to feel reassured that life still exists below. What stand for beaches on this volcanic island are strips of unnatural black soil.

"What's that?" I say, pointing to a white mass on the far end of the strip of land.

From far, it looks like a stray patch of snow with veins of black. As we drive closer, it's clear that it's something else entirely.

"Birds," says Antlop, who has better eyesight. "Albatross. Lots of seabirds around here."

He's right. But something looks off even with my mediocre vision. We stop the Toyota, and walk towards the morass of white and jagged black. The birds look too still, too quiet.

I've never seen an albatross colony. The birds are huge, their feathers a milky white with elegant black tips. But even I know that warm-blooded birds don't allow the wind to blow through their feathers like that, exposing the softest duvet and fragile appendages. Up close, we see their long wings are stiffened at odd angles, mangled, their bodies resting sideways. Their eyes are wide open, unblinking, and lackluster. They're all dead. Frozen. Only the feathers ruffle in the wind.

"What the hell?" says Antlop.

To see this after such an arduous crossing almost brings me to tears.

"It's as if they just died," I say, surprised that we're not smelling the stench even this close.

"The cold preserves things well here," says Antlop. "They could have died a while ago."

There's no blood and no sign of what killed them. Like they just dropped dead. I look around, but all I see is the other side of Ob Hill in the distance.

"What do you think happened? Can an entire colony collapse?"

"Never heard of something like this." Antlop shrugs.

There are no eggs. No fledglings. Antlop explains that they don't breed on Antarctica, but on the warmer islands surrounding it.

We're both starving and have fuel to make a fire. But we both know better than to try to eat any birds that died all of a sudden who knows how long ago. Fortunately the subject doesn't even come up.

It's not the sign of life we were hoping for. We trudge back to the Toyota in silence. Back at the station, we park near the bigger building, which at least has more doors to work with.

Swearing under my breath, I decide to wrench at all the doorknobs I find. I spot a camera perched high up above the entrance, recording everything.

"Is anybody there?" I shout, looking straight into the camera's eye. I kick the door several times with my boot for good measure.

I'm starting to get desperate. I look up at the sky,

wondering if we're on any flight path. We might find some discarded wood, and with the remaining fuel, we could build a fire, get a smoke signal up there. Didn't the depot attendant say there would be a flight out of Amundsen soon? Not for another few days though. Any amount of time is a long time to wait out here in the cold. I'm cursing and staring at the silent white sky, when I see something moving with my peripheral vision, up in one of the top windows. Something white, gray, and bulky. Then nothing. The problem is that it didn't look like a person.

"Did you see that?" I gasp.

"See what?" Antlop is so alarmed and entertained by the spectacle of my coming undone that he doesn't notice anything else.

It's hard to trust your mind in a place like this. I swear it looked like a giant, ambulatory snowman. That makes it very credible, indeed. Maybe my paranoia is back even though I'm taking the medication.

I start screaming, beating and kicking the door, all the while looking up at the same third-floor window. Antlop is now convinced that I've gone mad. Then I see it again: a white, amorphous figure moves furtively towards the window, then retreats just as quickly.

I'm terrified, but also elated. Maybe there is a blurb of news to report in this snowy hell hole, after all. Now I know it's not my imagination. Still, what can this white, hulking figure be? It fills me with curiosity and dread.

"What the hell is the matter with you?" says Antlop.

But before I can explain to him what I saw, the door I was kicking suddenly opens wide, and two towering white figures shove us to the ground, and drag us inside kicking.

28

Chen

It's Mielek who opens my eyes to the obvious. I just take the extra onion rings the Mexican cafeteria girl doles out to me every time they're on the menu.

"She wants you to ask her out," Mielek tells me. "So what are you waiting for?"

"What?" This is news to me.

"She doesn't give anybody else extra anything. She wants you to sleep with her," he says.

I chew on my burger, trying to put my head around this. A cute Hispanic chick wants to sleep with me—for free. I don't remember jack of my past, but I have a sneaky feeling that girls fawning over me was not part of it.

When I go take a piss after lunch, I stare at my face in the mirror. What does Enrika see in me? I'm not ugly, but I'm no prize either. My Asian skin got seriously pasty working in this dark dungeon. Then there's the embarrassing black orthopedic shoes they make us all wear. Meanwhile, the lunchroom babe has skin as smooth as a Milky Way, and her perky tits and flat tummy are a nice change from the old European blubber hanging at the museum. I just don't get it. Maybe she just thinks I'm too skinny and she's trying to fill me up with fried food. Mielek could be taking me for a ride telling me she has the hots for me. That bastard gets his thrills laughing at other people's expense.

I decide to pay a little more attention to Enrika the next day. This perks her up even more. She's sorry that onion rings aren't on the menu this time, and gives me a second cookie instead.

"How come I don't get an extra cookie?" Mielek whines. The creep never misses a thing.

"That extra belly of yours don't need no extra cookie," says Enrika.

Mielek smirks back.

"See how she treats you, and how she treats the rest of us? You're an idiot: you can't even see a girl in heat," he says when we've barely past her.

Still, she could just be fattening me up. I can definitely use some action though. After this sweat shop, getting it on with an old hooker four dress sizes bigger than me is not worth the trouble—or the dough. Still, I don't want to ask Enrika out in front of that prankster. I'm also not sure I know how. I think I'm better at planning a heist than a date.

Another two days of extra onion rings go by. I'm coming off my shift when I see Enrika hustling in front of me. Her stretch jeans show off her round, full ass in all its Mexican glory. I had no idea *that's* what was under the old nurse outfit they make the cafeteria girls wear. I catch up with her.

"Hey, you're staying late today," I say.

"Yeah, doin' overtime to train a new gal. So what's up with you?"

"Nothin' really," I say.

"Are you gonna ask me out, or are you just gonna eat my onion rings till the end of time?"

So that son of a bitch was right.

"I'm gonna do both," I say. "You free tomorrow night?"

"Sure." A giddy smile makes her face even prettier.

Enrika lives with her big familia: her silent, short, stocky padre and four of his offshoots—all gardeners. Her mother died of breast cancer. This means I have to be a good boy, or I'll have a tribe of angry men with hedge trimmers at my neck. It also means we won't be able to go back to her place after the movies. And she might get suspicious if I bring her back to my motel room. So I decide to take it slow, and just make out in the Hyundai that night. I'll have the week to find a place to move into. It's cheaper anyway. This whole artsy gig is taking a lot longer to wrap up. At least with the clean ID and the steady paychecks, I've got all the baloney that landlords want to see before they rent you their piece-of-shit place.

Enrika is happy to get a free dinner and movie without having to put out. She thinks I'm a nice guy who likes to take it slow and easy, unlike all the gang members she's used to. I just pocket the praise, drag my blue balls back to my motel room, and start looking for cheap rentals the next day.

. . .

Each time, I drive to a different library to research the artwork. To keep the nosy librarians out of my hair, I never check the art books out. I just read them right there, surrounded by retired grandpas who're looking for a warm body to talk to. If I'm gonna risk my hide for an old canvas rag with a bowl of fruit on it, it better be worth something to someone who's willing to cough up the cash. I'm doing so much homework that I end up buying those skinny glasses at the drugstore to avoid headaches. I sure hope this is my last gig 'cause it's already costing me enough self-respect.

After staking out my options, I settle on the baby Cézanne. It's a modest still life, but it has added value 'cause it's supposed to be the first gift Cézanne gave to his mistress, Hortense, who later finagled herself into becoming his wife. I look up what his oils fetched at Sotheby's and Christie's, and guestimate that the pomegranates and teacup could be worth a million on the black market. It isn't much by Impressionist standards, but it sure as hell goes a long way in Thailand. The biggest plus is that the painting isn't under glass or armed like some other snootier pieces.

Still, I have a lot of homework to do. Before I can come up with a good plan, I need to study those cameras. The cameras are so tiny these days that I can't even see where they are. I'll have to make a buddy in the control room, have beers with him after work, get him free baseball tickets, go visit him casually on my break once or twice, see how things work exactly, what shows up on their monitors. It's risky as hell, especially with Mielek eyeing every one of my moves, either because he was asked to, or because he's just a lonely parasite, living off of other people's joys and sorrows.

29

Max

Antlop and I kick and struggle as our two hulking abductors handcuff and frisk us in seconds. This is the last thing we expect at McMurdo. I understand then what I had seen moving near the upstairs window. A giant snowman would have been preferable. Instead, our two attackers are wearing white, Level-A HazMat suits with dark visors that render even the outline of their faces invisible. Despite the bulky suits and the thick gloves, they have superhuman strength and precision, judging by how quickly and effortlessly they subdue us. They breathe through a tank on their back, effectively avoiding all contact with the environment. I cringe at what this means. I just hope they're in the middle of some experiment or safety drill.

"Get this off me now," demands Antlop, shaking his handcuffs.

Gloved hands swiftly remove our watches and the

contents of our pockets, including the Toyota keys and Antlop's pocketknife.

Once we're no longer a threat, one of them slams the outside door shut. I'm in quiet, data-collection mode, trying to hear what the two tell each other through their in-suit two-way radio system. Never having stepped into a war zone, Antlop fights every step of the way.

"You can't do this," he tells them. "Antarctica is neutral. You have no authority here."

"Shut up," says one of the guys, who proceeds to tie a gag around Antlop's mouth.

Antlop gets on everybody's nerves, myself included, but still, it's a little excessive. I consider the situation. This is not your folksy bandana or ruthless duct tape, but a professional gag, one that passed clearance for humane treatment, the kind of thing the army spends money studying. These guys are not McMurdo lab rats testing how HazMat gear fares in subzero temperatures. Judging by their strength and efficiency, they have some serious military training.

It's actually a relief that Antlop can no longer put his foot in his mouth. I decide not to utter a word, unless they ask me a question. They play fair, and don't gag me. All in all, I prefer this outcome to hypothermia. You can't negotiate with the cold out there. At least our captors provide us with warm shelter—at last—and might even offer us some food. Paradoxically, it's energizing to have something newsworthy happening to me. I just hope I'll live long enough to write it up. That's always the rub with high drama.

"Who are you?" The faceless voice, trapped inside the helmet, sounds muffled.

I'm not in the mood to be interrogated on an empty stomach.

"Could you give us a little food while we talk? We haven't eaten for days," I say.

"This ain't a fucking diner," says the same fellow. Perfect American accent.

"I have a splitting headache too. Some coffee would really help," I say, unfazed.

"What else you want? Double shot mocha, extra whip?"

I refrain from nodding.

The fellow glances in the direction of the clock in the bare entrance, then makes a head gesture to his buddy, who leaves in silence. Clearly, they were in the middle of something, and running into us is an unwanted distraction.

"We'll get you some shit to eat. Now tell me what the fuck you're doing out here?"

Only the military can get away with this much cussing.

"They had no room in Amundsen, so they gave us a McMurdo vehicle to drive back here. We brought it back to you safely—and even paid for the fuel. We thought maybe you'd let us stay here for a couple of nights."

"Seriously?"

"Obviously a bad idea," I say.

"No shit. What did you come to the South Pole for?"

Sometimes being a journalist confers immunity, as everybody knows you have a big fat mouth that can get published in a big ass paper. But often, it's a death sentence. The problem is choosing heads or tails. I go with my gut. These guys, all bundled up in their suits, are up to something—perhaps just a military exercise—but still, reporters are the last people you'd want to see when you're doing something funny.

"We came here to study factors that accelerate the rate of ice crystal collapse," I say with a straight face. "Dr. Antlop here is a glaciologist from Iceland."

"And you? You got a PhD in bullshit?"

"Not yet. I'm Dr. Antlop's graduate student," I say.

Before the fellow can ask any more questions, his buddy

shows up with two heavy-duty plastic baggies for us. Inside, we find a machine-cut sandwich sealed in a plastic sleeve, applesauce in a sippy-like container, and a water packet with a built-in-spout. Astronaut food, stuff you can eat with minimal air contamination. So this may be more than today's safety drill. That's bad news.

"No coffee?" I ask.

"Sorry, nearest Starbucks is five thousand miles away," says the combative one.

The one who brought our food hands us two medication baggies, on which someone handwrote 'NoDoz.' There are two white caffeine pills in each pouch.

"It's the only form of caffeine we have." A woman's voice.

Antlop and I look up, surprised. I feel instantly better, even if I can't see a lick of her face or figure underneath her beekeeper outfit. All things being equal, I have better luck with women, that's a fact.

The girl walks up to Antlop, makes a signal for silence using her gloved index finger, where her invisible lips are, then removes the gag from his mouth so he can eat. The asshole of the two won't let us eat in peace, firing stupid questions at us, even though we're obviously famished. I ignore him and use the meal to think about what might be going on. Sooner or later, one of them might let something slip. Interrogators are often just as nervous as their prisoners, especially when the capture was not planned. Antlop and I feel less ill as soon as we've ingested some calories.

"Where are you from?" the relentless one asks me.

"I'm a US and French citizen," I say, not sure which confers better treatment here.

"Why did you try to break into the station?"

"We didn't want to die out in the cold."

"And why did you come here, anyway?"

I glare at Antlop, sensing that he might be more

dangerous with the gag off. Luckily, Antlop seems to have some newfound sense that we're better off if he kept his gob shut for once in his lifetime.

"I already told you why, to study the destruction of ice," I say.

"Why did you come *now*?"

"It's the start of the summer season: perfect weather for research."

"Yeah, right," the fellow says. "Who's funding the expedition?"

"National Science Foundation."

"You government?"

"Just using the tax dollars. Academics. Cornell University," I add.

There's a lull as the fellow runs out of questions. It's a good time for me to place one of my own.

"Say, are we safe without the gear?"

"I'm asking the questions here."

"Just a bit worried, that's all," I say.

"If you're worried about your health, you shouldn't have come here right now," he says.

I string the unsaid words together. 'Right now' implies there is some new danger other than the perpetual cold. Shit, they really are up to something that warrants Level A Haz-Mat suits.

"Chemical, biological, radiation? What should we be worried about?"

"Cut the chatter, will ya? Otherwise your number one worry is hypothermia." He says, flicking his chin toward the external door from which we'd come in.

Antlop stares on, alarmed, straining every muscle he has to avoid uttering a word. The interrogator makes a brisk head motion to his female colleague. They walk away to an adjacent hallway to powwow. They whisper to each other over their radio system, most likely to decide what to do with us. They're young and nervous. Front line fodder. It doesn't bode well for two nosy party-crashers.

As they walk back towards us, I overhear the fellow say something to the woman.

"I know it's better upstairs, but we're just not equipped for them there." He turns to us. "All right, on your feet, follow me. No more questions."

Antlop and I shuffle behind him, the girl flanking us at the rear, through long, empty hallways and dank stairs. We descend into a dark, cavernous basement, cluttered with whirring boilers, pumps, heaters, and piles of equipment. There isn't a single window down here. It smells of old dust and engine grease. They stop at what looks like the brig in the basement of McMurdo.

"Sorry, guys, but you got the 'go to jail card'," says the fellow.

"We didn't do anything. You can't jail us for no reason," says Antlop.

They ignore him.

We stop in front of two makeshift jails, with steel bars installed in a dead-end hallway, facing the same brick wall. Each cell has a toilet and a tiny sink. They unlock our handcuffs, shove us in separate cells, and turn off the lights.

"Hey, wait a minute, we have the right to a phone call," Antlop shouts after them.

"You're in Antarctica: you don't have the right to jack," says the asshole.

30

Chen

The studio apartment turns out to be a headache to find. I have to fork out a deposit—and the first and last month's rent. It leaves me broke and full of resentment. At least now I have a place to bring back Enrika for the night.

In bed, Enrika is nothing like the cafeteria girl. She's happy as can be in between the sheets. And sexy too—at least after I strip off her rainbow lingerie. Either it's a Mexican thing, or the candy pink and neon yellow were on sale. I'm not complaining about free sex with a clean, cuddly, and very motivated sex kitten though. She seems used to partying all night once she gets started. She doesn't have the weird self-hatred of white-trash chicks nursing their bruises at the bar. And she doesn't wear that bored, jaded look that the hookers can't wipe off their faces—even when the amnesia supposedly made them forget all their lousy old clients. Enrika likes to play in bed. The things she digs are kinda adolescent, like strawberry-scented condoms, edible body paint, or doing it in front of two mirrors. But, hey, I wanna make her happy too.

One time, wearing only a raincoat with nothing underneath, she asks me to put on my security guard uniform, pick her up at the local diner, take her home, snap velvet handcuffs on her, and fuck her brains out. I'm not so crazy about the idea.

"No way, man, it's a little too close to home," I blurt out.

"What do you mean?" She looks worried—it's the first time I say no to one of her fantasies.

I backtrack.

"Well, I mean, I don't want to do this kind of stuff so close to where I live. You know, if the neighbors recognize us or something."

She pouts. She doesn't understand that's what I saw on my record, what got me in the slammer: I must've picked up some girl at a bar, who was drunk in a puddle of grief, and, let's face it, really there just to get some company. The next morning, it's her word against mine—and we all know women can lie better than men. The only difference today is the security guard badge. It makes Enrika think she knows me. Who knew a forty-dollar uniform could have so much frickin' power over the female brain?

Later that night, when Enrika falls asleep curled against my chest, I stay up, staring at my own rented ceiling. I wonder what she'll think when she hears I stole a painting and hit the runway to Bangkok. Sure, she'll cry. Then she'll probably start buttering up the next new guard with extra treats.

Lying on my IKEA bed with a steady girlfriend in my arms, I'm getting way too comfortable in this phase of the operation. I'd better start hatching serious plans. Part of the hiccup is that without an accomplice I can't pull the wool over the cameras and bolt out of an armed exit. Enrika is too soft to help with this kind of stuff—and I don't wanna get her in trouble. The other guards are family people who need to stick around to feed their children. The janitor is too old and decrepit for this shit. The only person left is Mielek.

I just wish the guy wasn't so creepy. I don't know if I could trust Mielek to be in on this. I'd give anything to know his past life. Was he a prison guard back home? Did he dump bodies in mass graves? Mielek might agree to team up, then turn me in. Or he could throw me off a boat in Phuket and keep all the dough for himself.

Still, if Mielek had it in for me, he would've already told our gray-haired boss lady that I don't belong here. Maybe he's letting me stay 'cause he suspects I'm up to something —and 'cause he *wants* to be part of the action. I have to get to know him a bit more before I show my hand. First, I need to find out if he has a lady friend, since women always complicate a man's life.

I pick the time when Mielek is cool and relaxed, when he's chain-smoking out back after lunch.

"Hey, man, do you have a girlfriend, so we can double date sometime?" I say.

"Why, you need help keeping Enrika happy?" He smirks.

"Nah, I got that covered."

"Call me if you need an extra hand—or an extra, you know." He grabs his crotch.

"Bug off," I say, rolling my eyes. "So did you come to the US with anybody?"

"Nobody."

"They give you a green card or something?"

"I convinced US immigration that I was a victim back in the war." His wincing laugh looks like a heart attack, but I know better now.

"So did you ever figure out what you were doing back then?"

"Probably what everybody was doing back then: killing people just to survive." With that weird smile, I can't tell if he's serious or joking.

"Uh-huh." I try to keep calm, like I couldn't care less. I chew on one of my cold onion rings to ease the tension. "You like it here, man, or do you miss home?"

"Better to forget it. Now I'm in America. I have to pay taxes, avoid deportation, and listen to the big boss lady, even if I really want to cut her into pieces, grind her into sausage, and feed her to the cats."

I almost choke. Never did an onion ring taste so rotten.

31

Max

In the gloom of the basement, I wake up groggy, unsure if it's day or night. My head throbs, probably because I stopped the opioid replacement pills cold turkey. If I tell our captors that I need the meds in the Toyota, they'll search my stuff. It could also be the effect of some mysterious contaminant. Best not to dwell on that.

Antlop is snoring away in the adjacent cell. All the machines that keep the building running are housed down here: power generators, snow melters, furnaces, and hot water boilers. The engines generate a constant racket—and a suffocating heat. I wonder if all this combustion produces carbon monoxide, which could also explain my migraine.

Sadly, what weak light there is comes from the red and green on and off switches on the machines. On top of the dust and grease, I smell pungent disinfectant. As much as I tired of the blinding sun madly reflecting off the ice, I now miss it. Even the ice-cold air shocking my throat and lungs is so much better than the dark and noisy bowels of this dungeon.

The shadow of a figure dances on the wall facing my jail cell. I stand up, uncertain whom I'll be dealing with, the asshole, the girl, or yet another one of them. It's her, I can tell from her smaller stature and movements, which are just as awkward with the gear, but not as abrupt as the guy's. She slides a see-through plastic pouch through the gap between the floor and the steel bars. Inside is another pre-fabricated meal—and another two pills.

"What are these?" I say, not so convinced they're caffeine pills, because they neither helped my headache nor kept me awake.

"Medication," she says.

"For what?"

"All you need to know is that your life depends on them."

So the meds have something to do with the contamination. That's very reassuring.

"The least you can do is tell us what we're going to die of," I say.

"We're not stupid. We got your passports from the truck —and your press badge. You're a journalist and Antlop is your prop. Don't lie next time."

At that, she leaves. Fucking press badge. I don't know why we even bother. Gone are the days when reporters were untouchable. This makes our release a dim prospect. Antlop is still in his coma-level sleep. His time is better spent asleep —for his sake and mine. I ingest the calories—because calling it a meal is a stretch—and use the quiet time to think about our options.

Even if we manage to escape from the brig, it's not like there's an embassy to run to out there. The French base is quite far away—if it's open at all. The soldiers have surely stowed the Toyota away, which in any case has too little fuel left for an escape back to any of the bases. And if Brownell inquires about us, our captors can deny ever having seen us. Over the course of a thousand-mile drive through Antarctica, we could have easily slipped into a crevasse—or gotten off road and been buried by the snow. It's a continent, after all. Basically, Antlop and I depend entirely on these foot soldiers, whatever they're busy doing out here.

When Antlop wakes up, he's in a crabby mood. He despairs in the adjacent cell, alternately blaming me for bringing him here, and hatching escape plans that completely ignore the obvious obstacles, inside and outside of McMurdo. Now that they know I'm a reporter, I expect another interrogation, especially from the nasty fellow. Instead, no one shows up. It's almost disappointing. As a prisoner, you have a love-hate relationship with your jailors. On the one hand, you don't want to see them, because that can bring confrontation and pain. On the other hand, not seeing them makes you nervous, because paradoxically, they become your surest ticket to freedom.

The next time someone shows up, it's the asshole.

"You leave us in total darkness, like cattle." Antlop shakes an angry finger at him. "You have no authority to lock us up without charges. This is grossly inhumane treatment. You'll be prosecuted in the Hague."

"We have orders to do what we see fit with you, you understand?" says the soldier from behind his visor.

"And why aren't you giving us protective gear to wear?" says Antlop.

"Because, frankly, you're more inconvenient alive than dead."

Chances are he's telling us the truth. Maybe we also make good guinea pigs, so they can study the effects of the contaminant on us. Despite the mean talk, the fellow produces a bigger meal than usual, with extra water and peanut butter packets for us to keep in the cell to eat later. The tone is more abusive, but the treatment is better. I try to take advantage of this.

"Can't you leave a little light on once in a while? So at least we know day from night?" I say.

"No."

"Why not?"

"Shut up."

"Can you let us shower?" I ask.

"We don't have time for this shit," the soldier grumbles. "Wash up in your sink."

"We haven't bathed since New York," I say softly. "You're breathing from a tank. But we stink in here."

I need a shower, of course, but I also want to get my bearings around the basement, map the locations of doors and staircases.

It's the girl who supervises our showers, one at a time. The basement shower stall is the kind found in chemistry labs, for the purpose of rinsing off in the event of a chemical spill. The shower curtain is translucent. She doesn't turn her visor away when I undress or bathe. I'm not sure what to make of it, but I don't let it ruin my ten minutes of hot water and suds.

When I'm done, she hands me an orange jumpsuit. It's hard to tell with her visor, but I could swear she's staring at my crotch. Whatever, anything, if it brings us closer to getting out of here. I feel more civilized after bathing, though I'm not happy about wearing prison garb that's easy to detect against the snow, should we attempt a suicidal escape. I extend my hand to get my dirty street clothes back. She shakes her helmeted head and keeps our stuff. She's a tough cookie. While the girl soldier accompanies me back to my cell, I try to get as much as I can out of her.

"What happened here?" I ask.

"We're not going there," she says categorically.

"How long will you keep us in here?"

"Until you become too much of a pain in the ass."

"I thought we're already a pain in the ass," I say. "Look, let us drive back to Amundsen or the French Dumont d'Urville base. We'll reimburse you for the fuel, and we'll pretend we never met you."

"It's too late for that," she says ominously.

32

Max

After the shower excursion, Antlop and I compare notes about what we saw on the way there and back. We create a mental map of the basement, and start a log of our captors' habits. The soldier keeps the keycard to our jail cells in her hip pocket. She needs it to open the cells, but not to lock them. The proximity card reader pad is just out of reach from our cell doors. We discuss the heavy equipment and various electric tools we saw. An old snowplow in need of repairs suggests there is a sloped driveway to the outside, through which the giant thing had been rolled in. We counted three power generators; a snow melter; a good number of heating boilers, some running on jet fuel and some sitting idle as back-ups; an incinerator for the building's trash; and boxes and boxes of what look like new replacement parts, should any of these vital machines break down. Fluorescent lights hang all over the basement ceiling, turned off. They're keeping us in the dark on purpose, literally and figuratively.

～

With the oppressive darkness down here, there is little to distinguish day from night. Not only did our jailors remove our watches, but they refuse to tell us what time it is, keeping us disoriented. They also avoid normal greetings like "good morning" or "goodnight," or even "here's your breakfast or dinner." Antlop and I are sleepy and lethargic all the time. We're already suffering from cabin fever—if not from some serious contamination syndrome.

It's the nasty one who drops off our meal packets this time, then escapes before answering any of my questions. Without telling Antlop, I decide not to swallow the pills in my food bag. It'll be interesting to see what worse symptoms I might develop without the medication. It's information like any other—I just hope it won't kill me. Maybe if I fall ill, it'll force them to do a medical evacuation. I save the pills in the seam of my jumpsuit, in case I chicken out and decide to take them.

I pace to pass the time, though I can't make more than three steps in any direction. Soon after our meal, Antlop falls silent. I call to him, but the fellow must have fallen asleep already. If we're still on our old circadian rhythm, that would make it dinner time, I reason, though I'm not feeling particularly sleepy myself. I try to make sense of the little I learned so far. There must be a reason they're keeping us imprisoned, instead of sending us packing on the next plane. Are planes even flying in and out of McMurdo? It's been a struggle to hear the outside sounds beyond the purring of the engines. I'm pretty sure I haven't heard a plane in the skies since we got here. That Amundsen-Scott bureaucrat implied that there were no scheduled flights to McMurdo, which is very odd, as McMurdo is the bigger station usually supporting the smaller one in the South Pole.

Providing even minimal care to their prisoners seems to be a burden for the soldiers. So far, Antlop and I have only met the two who'd been assigned to deal with us. Surely, there are many more people at McMurdo—usually in the hundreds in the winter and up to a thousand coming in for the summer. There has to be at least a third person, the figure I'd seen moving in the upstairs window right before the other two abducted us from the ground floor.

It's been impossible to decipher the soldiers' faces through their helmets. I can only go by their height, gait, behavior, their responses to inquiries, and the little emotion that seeps through their stifled voices. They seem fatigued, their nerves frayed. They are quick to lose their patience, and they easily resort to hostility, especially the guy. It's the reactivity of people under stress. Having not much else to go by, I lie down on my cot, pull a fleece blanket all the way to my neck, and try to sleep.

When I sense a light flickering over my closed eyelids, I fight against the temptation to open them. I remain still and feign sleep. The light soon retreats. I open my eyes just enough to see one of the soldiers shining a flashlight in Antlop's cell, probably ascertaining that he's asleep too. What are they up to now?

Soon I hear a new set of sounds superimposed on the background of engines noises. Feet shuffle around—not those of two people, but several. There's a glow of faint, erratic lights reflected on the wall facing our cells. Flash-lights or lights installed atop helmets is my guess. A heavy door creaks open somewhere in the basement. I feel a cold gust moments later. It's a door to the outside, bringing in wafts of crisp clean air into my nostrils, fresh on my cheeks. It feels divine.

I strain to hear other noises. They whisper through their radios, too low to distinguish. Then I hear the screeching of wheels on concrete. I'm convinced this will wake up Antlop, if it hasn't already. I stand close to our shared wall, poised to hush him, so we can learn something from the commotion. Surprisingly, Antlop remains oblivious.

The sounds settle into a repetitive pattern: the outside door opens; the wheeled cart screeches; the outside door closes; more wheeling around; then another door opens—an inside, metallic door—then what sounds like unloading of a heavy object—before the metallic door closes. Sometime later—perhaps half an hour—the inside door reopens and closes, after more unloading. Then the cycle reverses: the cart is wheeled back to the outside door, and it begins all over again.

They must be bringing in heavy loads from the outside, on wheeled carts, into the basement. My first guesses have to do with some routine aspect of the harsh life in Antarctica: barrels of heating fuel; barrels of snow to melt into water; food supplies; equipment. There is a stronger smell of combustion than usual, as well as a vague stench that sometimes wafts in here along with the clean air, as though the garbage might be stored just outside the door they keep opening. Fortunately, the air that has traversed the continent and the ocean brings with it the freshness of snow, neutralizing both smells.

I have hours to tally every possibility. Then I recall the flashlight one of the soldiers shone on our faces before they started the nocturnal hubbub. They wanted to make sure their prisoners were asleep first, which means it's no routine task like loading up fuel for the boilers. They're clearly hiding something.

The frenzy lasts all night, it seems. Soon after the activity dies down, I fall asleep, exhausted.

33

Chen

It's a pretty quiet afternoon when I'm assigned to the Impressionist galleries. I drool over the plush cash cushion that my buddy Cézanne will bring me someday. I just gotta iron out the right exit strategy. I bought a backpack big enough to hold the painting, filled it with symbolic workout gear, and placed it in my locker. I've settled on the emergency exit off the cafeteria, 'cause it would put me closer to the street. On beverage delivery days, that exit is propped open, unarmed till the boys finish stowing the drinks in the coolers. If I'm the guard assigned to supervise the delivery, maybe I can figure out a way to keep the alarm on that door disabled till shortly before closing. Still, it's tricky. Problem is still those pesky cameras 24/7.

Right then, I notice a white patron staring at me. I stand up straight and act like the invisible security guard they like to see around here. The fellow leaves his platinum-blond lady-friend near the Renoir, and starts walking over to me in big bold steps. Do I know this guy? All white people look the same to me. He starts talking to me, calling me sir.

"Excuse me, sir, you might want to check that gallery over there. A kid was touching the Degas sculpture and we thought you oughta know."

I thank him and run to the room next door. Sure enough, there's only one patron there, a teenager swaggering from the bronze Degas girl, toward the baby Cézanne. Time-honored stereotypes tell me this white kid is not one of the usual artist-wannabes, who never touch the art, because that would be blasphemy. Those artsies have a uniform of their own too. They always carry a sketchpad like they'll simply die without one. Their pants or shoes have to be striped, paint-stained, or a strange shape. And they have a thing for rabid bed hair. This piece of white trash belongs squarely in the 'hood: baggy pants, unwashed hoodie, and a whiff of something cheap and illegal, like meth. The second he sees me, he drops his eyes. He's up to something.

Then I get it. The kid's seeing blood: he looks at the Cézanne like he's about to pick a fight with it. He's going for the weakest thing in the room, the one painting with no protection. Then, before I can come up with something to say—because we're really trained to just keep our mouth shut—I see the box cutter flashing in his hand. This snotty teenager is about to ruin my ticket to retirement.

I do the first thing that comes to mind: I tackle the little punk, restrain his right arm against his wiry body. He struggles to free his weapon. I call for reinforcement, but no one hears me. The kid has more strength than I expected for his frame. With meth on board, he doesn't even feel pain. I can't keep his arm secured for long, and I can't make him drop the box cutter either.

Next thing you know, we're rolling around the floor

together, grunting like animals, gripping each other where we can, arms, legs, neck. Blood smears everywhere. His blood. My blood. Who knows. I'm no good at this. I get nicked and pierced by the blade. Warm stuff leaks out of me, from what places, I can't even tell 'cause we're rolling around the hardwoods and everything hurts. The meth-head holds my arm down and jams his blade right into my hand like it's just another slab of butter. The pain is a bitch. I close my eyes tight, knowing what's coming. I feel another burning jab, this time in my arm. As the cutter digs into my neck, I glance one last time at my baby on the wall, 'cause I worry she's next. I feel the blood draining out of me. I really worked hard for this, man. It's too bad I'm gonna die trying.

34

Max

When I wake up, Antlop is already awake, accepting a breakfast delivery from a new guy. The vague smell of cleaner clings in the air.

"Sorry for the delay," says this third soldier in HazMat gear.

It comforts me to hear a new, calmer voice—and an apology, for a change. A sign of empathy, perhaps. I jump at the opportunity to get something out of this guy.

"No worries, we know you're short-staffed," I say.

"Ain't that the truth," replies the soldier. I detect a tone that could be African-American, but I'm not sure.

"Say, how long do you plan to keep us here?"

The soldier turns his visor away and leaves, without a response. I memorize his movements: more at ease in his body than the other two, his upper body broader than the first guy.

Of course, Antlop is just as let down as I am that the appearance of this new soldier didn't do anything to increase our chances of being released.

"So now that we're locked up for who knows how long, can you tell me why the hell we came here?" says Antlop, despondent.

"We came here to follow a lead related to the amnesia," I whisper. "But maybe we've stumbled on something else entirely."

Antlop scoffs, then grumbles in Icelandic, like he's followed a madman off a cliff.

Despite being at the mercy of these secretive people, and exposed to some mysterious toxic agent, for the first time since we've been dragged in here, I feel like my normal self —or as close to it as I can remember. The headache, grogginess, and lethargy are all gone. Maybe I'm not in withdrawal anymore. Still, I expected to feel worse skipping their antidote, not better. In the breakfast pouch, I find the usual two pills. From the seam of my jumpsuit I retrieve last night's dinner pills, and compare them with the breakfast pills. Same color, same shape, but different numbers. They're giving us two different drugs. I quietly skip the breakfast pills too, and stow them in a different hiding place. I don't tell Antlop: he's my blind control group.

It's the bad-tempered one who brings us dinner and dodges our questions. I eat the food, but stash the medication away. After dinner, Antlop gets groggy right in the middle of a conversation about Icelandic women. This isn't normal: the guy loves to go on and on about anything Icelandic. His words slur a bit, then he falls asleep abruptly. It hits me then: we're being sedated—at least at night. The morning pills may be antidotes, but in the evening, they're feeding us sleeping pills, so that we're oblivious to all the nocturnal commotion. I pretend to doze off.

The same pattern unfolds not long after dinner. One of the soldiers shines a light on our faces to make sure we're out, then the same repetitive noises rattle off. The shuffle goes on for hours. There are periodic shifts in the temperature of the basement, from cold wafts when the outside door is opened, to hotter than usual dry heat during the loading. During each new cycle, I try to dissect every sound, which I have to separate from the background murmur of the machines. I focus my energies on the most informative sound: the inner metallic door, which they open and close, each time they load something into it. There are occasional metallic scraping noises too. Why do they wait for an interlude of about half an hour in between loads? And why do they close the door each time, rather than propping it open for convenience?

Each time the inside door opens, I make out a faint sound distinct from the other background noises, like an emphysemic breath. The sound of flames, of a flow of gas combusting. That explains the heating of the basement during the operation, the stronger smell of exhaust. If it were just snow being melted, it would smell cleaner in here, not so dry on the nostrils. It occurs to me that they could be loading waste into the incinerator. That's why they don't prop the inside door wide open, as cumbersome as it is to open and close it each time. It would get too hot in here and waste energy. The periodic scraping noises could be the scooping of ash out of the incinerator.

But burning trash is not something they'd bother hiding from us. They must be destroying large stacks of documents or data—or maybe even deactivating chemical or biological agents. Hence the protective gear, as bulky and hot as it must be. That's also why each load takes time to incinerate.

A crashing noise echoes in the air, like something heavy falling on the concrete—and breaking into pieces. It almost sounds like a block of ice. I hear raised voices inside the helmets, some loud enough to be audible.

The female soldier's voice is emphatically calm.

"It's OK. It's all right," she says.

The bad-tempered one shouts loudly.

"Nothing's fucking all right."

"Get a hold of yourself. No need to lose it, man. We gotta finish the job." It's the even, firm voice of the third soldier.

"Broken bag. Disinfectant, stat," orders the girl.

She could be a physician or paramedic. All I can think of is biological stockpiles of who knows what, something that has to be deactivated with disinfectant, or it can cause infection.

"I didn't sign up for this shit." It's the nasty one, raw rage in his voice.

"Cut it out, man. None of us signed up for this." It's the third guy again, his tone soft.

More frantic loading. The inside door opens and closes.

I'm hoping it's not an airborne agent, but it could well be, given that they're all carrying oxygen tanks. Reluctantly, I sniff the air, before the industrial disinfectant drowns everything out. I'm expecting some unfamiliar biological smell, or perhaps the odor of the chemical solution used as its medium.

Instead, it's the unmistakable stench of death—like animals decomposing. I immediately think of the colony of dead albatross. Why would they bother with a bunch of dead birds? Dead monkeys from a classified experiment?

Experimental animals would just as easily have been flung into the ocean to be eaten by the fish—unless they had been infected by a highly contagious agent. Then, they would need to be destroyed in the incinerator. The only reason I haven't smelled them before is that they're bagged—and frozen from being outside.

35

Chen

I'm feeling weak and delirious. My head is aching, and my face is flat on the ground. I hear a storm of footsteps. Finally, the camera guys must've gotten off their asses and sounded the alarms. Mielek, Dieguito, and Gumphrey all run over. Mielek's stainless steel eyes home in on us like missiles. He shoves the little shit away from me, making him land hard on the floor. With his heavy boot, Mielek crushes the kid's forearm with all his weight, forcing him to release the blade. It takes all three of them to subdue the good-for-nothing and snap handcuffs on him. I recover my breath and take a look at the damage. Blood's dripping from my hand and my arm from two deep gashes. Gumphrey holds a handkerchief to a slit in my neck. I feel real queasy now at the sight of all this blood pouring out of my body. Then I hear the police sirens, and that just puts me over the edge. I pass out in Gumphrey's arms.

· · ·

When I come to in the ambulance, I can't believe I'm not the one that the cops hauled away. Two paramedics hover over me like I'm Old Getty's precious little heir, making sure I'm comfy under a warm blanket, telling me that I'm all safe now in their capable hands. At the hospital, they stitch me up, and the nurses shower me with TLC and feed me orange juice and saltines. The doc tells me that if the gash in my neck had been just half an inch to the left, the prick would have snipped an artery and I might have bled to death. Basically, I got fucking lucky.

36

Max

What I've witnessed, heard, and smelled troubles me. I'm too keyed up to sleep in the few remaining quiet hours. They can't possibly be sedating us against our will just to dispose of infected experimental animals.

Another possibility comes to mind. It would explain the secretiveness, the need for a cart—and the soldiers' distress when the bag fell and tore open. What if they're incinerating human corpses, to hide evidence of a classified experiment with biological agents that ended tragically? Human remains are difficult to dispose of without a trace. Even human skulls at the bottom of the sea could eventually be discovered and investigated—given the thousands of scientists studying this continent every year. That could be why our captors are frightened of a journalist, and short-tempered after an exhausting, Macbethian night of gore. Antlop and I are more than a nuisance: we pose a real threat to their cover-up. It's a miracle that they haven't eliminated us yet.

When Antlop wakes up, I try not to let my worry show. But he senses my irritability, my sulky mood.

"You said that we're risking our lives for something meaningful. Where is it then?" demands Antlop.

He keeps demanding answers, but then he's so easily flustered by the answers that it can bring on more trouble. As little confidence as I have in the Icelandic's judgment at times, the guy did save my life out there. He brought the engine back to life, and maneuvered our vehicle away from the crevasse masterfully and calmly. We're in this together. And in many ways, it's my fault that we're imprisoned. The least I can do is tell him about the sedatives, so he has the choice about whether to be medicated or not.

The girl shows up with our breakfast, a mere few hours after she had to clean up the mess when the body bag broke open. I act appropriately groggy and choose my words carefully to inquire about something neutral: our next opportunity to shower. She sounds tired, noncommittal. Our cleanliness is the last thing on her mind. After she leaves and I hear the stairwell door close, I whisper to Antlop.

"I think the pills they're giving us at night are sedatives."

Antlop is incensed merely by this possibility—he doesn't even know the rest of it.

"How dare they sedate us without our consent," he says. "I thought I was taking an antidote, not a sedative."

He decides to continue taking the breakfast pills only, which he still believes are antidotes. I intend to keep skipping all the medication. We agree to compare notes on symptoms.

Then he asks the obvious question I should have expected.

"Why the hell would they be sedating us?"

He'll keep pestering me if I don't answer him. So I tell him about what I heard and smelled without making extrapolations.

"I think they're incinerating those dead albatross," I say.

"Why would they do that?"

"Maybe an experiment gone bad."

Antlop is horrified even by this. He doesn't want to believe me, but I know he does, because he paces and grumbles for the rest of the day. He agrees that we need to obtain more information before jumping to conclusions. Antlop's second opinion would be welcome right now, given that I've had my share of paranoia lately.

"Promise to let me handle the questioning, no matter what," I say.

"What if I have a few questions myself?" he asks, unhappy with my gag order.

"Remember, I'm the journalist trained in interviewing people. I'm also used to dealing with soldiers. You can't ask them any question, just because you think you have a right to the answer. Here, they have absolute authority over us."

"Fine, fine," he says.

It takes extreme discipline to act like we know nothing. It's clear to me from the previous night that the soldiers are not just overworked and sleep-deprived, but traumatized too. Something terrible has happened here, and the soldiers we see are either survivors or the unlucky clean-up crew. Some of the dead could have been their buddies. They're keeping the bodies outside in the cold, either because that's where they had died, or because it's a natural morgue of sorts—or both. They're doing this in the dimmer parts of the circadian cycle to keep their activities less visible to potential spy satellites. It must be difficult to keep anything hidden in the constant Antarctic light.

I must choose whom to approach first for some delicate

questioning. I decide against the Spartan girl, who apparently can stomach a lot and definitely has a cold edge—she might even be a young surgeon. She's the type to kill you for asking the wrong question. As for the apologetic, even-keeled one, he's almost too resilient, the perfect soldier who can follow orders and let the gore slide off him like Teflon. He has no inner motivation to stray from rules and regulations. Paradoxically, the most vulnerable of the three is the caustic one, the asshole. He was the only one to break down and protest when the body bag ripped open and revealed its gruesome contents. It takes someone who's angry at the rules to break them. But he worries me. He can be explosive.

~

The soldier's footsteps echo off the wall facing our cells. It's time. The nocturnal commotion will soon begin. Antlop's first challenge is to make sure he keeps his eyes closed when the soldier comes around with the flashlight.

How Antlop will take what he hears tonight worries me. Part of me hopes that he'll keep thinking it's just albatross. Right after the soldier with the flashlight leaves, Antlop begins pacing frantically. Another night of loading bodies rolls by, this time with Antlop hearing it all, and smelling the exhaust, the disinfectant, and the few whiffs of stench that travel our way. The more he hears, the more I worry about his indignant reactivity, that he'll start yelling at any moment, risking a confrontation with them. I whisper to him that he must remain absolutely silent, that their nerves are already threadbare.

All the whispering and pacing sparks their suspicions. Next thing we know, we hear footsteps walking briskly toward us. I barely have time to get back under the covers and shut my eyes, before one of them waves a flashlight over my face again. I just hope Antlop has the wherewithal to feign sleep too, that he manages to keep himself under control. The soldier inspects Antlop's cell for an unusually long time.

Miraculously, Antlop manages to keep it all in. I know he won't last all night though, as it's slowly dawning on him that it could be worse than dead seabirds. Right after the soldier leaves, I convince him that we should both swallow the sedatives to sleep through the racket.

37

Max

By morning, Antlop is uncharacteristically silent, aloof, lost in a very dark place. I let him be, give him time to process.

"They're burning bodies," he says at last.

"We don't know that for sure," I say weakly. So it's not just my paranoia.

It's the bad-tempered one who brings our breakfast. He's about to turn away in his characteristic brisk step, when I address him.

"So how come the three of you are doing all the dirty work?" I say.

Quietly, the soldier considers the many possible meanings of my hook.

"What do you mean dirty work?" he snaps, predictably aggressive.

"Well, you're taking care of us down here—but you're also stuck mopping up whatever contamination you're worried about," I say.

"Mind your own fucking business," he spits through his visor.

I expected as much, but I notice that the soldier hasn't aborted the conversation, so I press on, hoping Antlop will stay quiet in his cell.

"We're going to die anyway, so why not tell us who we have to thank for it?"

"Why don't you just figure it out for yourself, asshole?" he says.

Quietly, I wait for a few precious pearls from him, when Antlop, who's been listening the whole time, interjects.

"I can't believe you—"

"Antlop!" I warn him, reminding him of our deal.

After what he heard the night before, this is the last straw for Antlop.

"What did you do here? What exactly are you incinerating? What are you hiding?" Antlop screams at the soldier, all his repressed rage bursting out.

"Shut up, shut the fuck up," shouts the soldier.

"Antlop, stop it," I say, trying to drown out what else he's blurting out.

Nothing can stop Antlop on his rant.

"It's against the treaty. You will be prosecuted," he says.

"The old farts were right: we should've left you out there in the cold from day one," says the soldier, seething, and now afraid of the big ruckus that this is making.

"Who did you murder?" shouts Antlop.

At that, the soldier opens Antlop's cell.

"Don't touch me," yells Antlop.

I hear what sounds like a painful punch, a grunt, then a thud when Antlop falls over. Then the clinking of handcuffs. The soldier drags the Icelandic professor by the legs, through the hallway, leaving a trail of blood behind.

"You'll regret this," shouts Antlop.

"Please, he's just afraid of dying, just like you and me," I say, but my pleas are useless.

"We've fucking had enough of him," says the soldier. "You all shouldn't have come here. We didn't need this shit."

"Please, you gave him a warning, now just leave him here," I say.

Antlop turns to me, his nose bloody, an absolute terror in his eyes.

"Don't let them get away with this," he tells me, his words slurred by his swelling face.

"Shut up," shouts the soldier, lugging him away.

I can no longer see them, but I can hear the handcuffs scraping the concrete floor, and Antlop protesting and swearing.

The outside door creaks open. A dull gray light reflects off the wall facing me. Antlop is kicked out in the cold, screaming. Then I hear the outside door slamming shut.

I expect the soldier to come back for me. He just shouts at me from the hallway.

"If you don't keep your gob shut, you're next."

"Please, I know you're just following orders. He's angry at them, not you. It's just the strain of being locked up." I try to engage him again, convince him to bring back Antlop before it's too late, that we won't tell anybody anything. But the soldier slams the door to the stairwell behind him.

I'm hoping this is just a warning, a lesson, and that the broken soldier will come back in twenty minutes to fetch Antlop and stuff him back in his cell.

I keep shouting for them to come back and help Antlop, my voice hoarse, my screams ignored. No one hears me. Or no one cares. It occurs to me that the soldier didn't deny Antlop's accusations, didn't feed him some other explanation.

None of the soldiers comes to save Antlop. Nobody

comes back down to the basement for what feels like a hundred years.

It's the darkest day of the incarceration. With his handcuffs, Antlop scratches and bangs on the metal door—denouncing them till the very end. I try to comfort him. I tell him how sorry I am for bringing him here, that he won't die in vain, because the truth will come out eventually. Sadly, he doesn't seem to hear anything I say from so far away, with doors, walls, and machines between us. He just mutters and bangs his handcuffs on the metal doorknob, trying to break the chain, to no avail. With no coat, no gloves, no hat, he can't last long. I have no idea what the weather is like out there, sunny and calm, or windy and treacherous. I know the cold is claiming his nose, ears, toes and fingertips first, then working its way into his heart and his brain. Once more, all I can do is witness another man dying.

"Criminal," is Antlop's last audible utterance.

38

Max

I sit in the sudden silence, in the dark basement, listening. Sifting through the morass of words Antlop emitted over the course of our trip, I remember what he told me about his two boys and his wife. Antlop was someone's father, someone's husband. I feel terrible for pulling him into this mess. He was an academic, used to lecturing about amusing cultural idiosyncrasies. I should have known that he was an idealist—one for whom the truth can be lethal. He was better off sedated.

Their coldhearted abandonment of Antlop out there should have come as no surprise to me. Who knows the extent of what they're covering up. They had nights and nights of this—well before we got here. That explains why there are no flights between McMurdo and Amundsen. The damage must be extensive. Not just a few, but more than twenty bodies. If all of McMurdo's wintering scientists were affected, then it's over a hundred bodies. These are the same soldiers who'd had to pull who knows how many of their colleagues' bodies out of the buildings, or dig them out of the snow, and stack them outside in the icy cold. These are the same damaged souls who had to see each of their buddies' frozen faces before bagging them. Could this just be my imagination, my rampant paranoia again?

At this moment, I too am better off sedated, even if it's daytime. I fish out the four sleeping pills I stashed away, and wash them all down with a water packet. I keep the supposed antidote pills untouched. I'm now convinced they're a placebo—or something ineffectual like aspirin. Do they even know *what* killed these people? How can they have medication to treat the effects of something they must not have intended? Could whatever happened here be related to the amnesia? Does it explain why the emergency calls started in the southernmost tips of countries in the Southern hemisphere?

Even in sleep, I find no reprieve. In my nightmares, I hear every single one of Antlop's pleas once more—and that horrid sound of metal grating on metal.

When I finally wake up, my head is leaden and my mouth cobwebby. The double dose of sleeping pills knocked me out. One of the soldiers must have left a meal pouch under my door. I inspect the numbers on the pills. It's the sedatives: I'm supposed to be sleeping again soon. I try to swallow some food, but my stomach feels like a solid ball after what happened to Antlop. I gulp the water, then hide the pills. I settle on my cot and pretend to sleep. It's not long before the nocturnal commotion begins again—with the flashlight waved over my eyelids.

What I dread happens first.

"Start with the Icelandic," says the Spartan girl.

I stifle my tears as I hear Antlop's fresh body being carted in from outside, loaded into the flames, and the incinerator door slammed shut. My heart shatters into a thousand pieces. I want to scream, but I know if I do, I'll be next—and we will both have died without delivering the truth. I reach for a packet of water and down the two sedatives they'd given me.

39

Chen

When the Getty staff replay the security cameras, they're shocked and awed by my street instincts. I could have just followed protocol: sound the alarm and call for reinforcement. Instead, without thinking twice, I did what was best for the painting—and worst for me: I tackled a nutcase brandishing a blade.

Turns out, my baby Cézanne suffered only a tiny speck of damage: a few drops of my blood sprayed the painting. The museum immediately flew over a team of experts all the way from Italy to dab away the stains for a fat fee. I'm happy that they were able to clean it up, but I can't help thinking my blood got mixed up with some of the most expensive paint on Earth. Me and the pomegranates are forever blood brothers.

The cottony director lady who hired me gives a little speech about my "amazing bravura" in front of all the other guards. She hands me an employee-of-the-year award, and quietly drops a ten-thousand-dollar bonus into my account. I'm convinced the bank made a dumb mistake in my favor so I keep mum about it—until I get the Getty letter about a cash award for outstanding performance under pressure. They even promote me to Security Guard 2. Enrika is so proud of me that she walks around with a silly smile stuck on her face for a week. Every night while I'm recuperating, she comes over to cook me soup and insists on doing my laundry.

The incident is picked up by the press. I'm recovering at home, on paid leave, still bandaged up, when I see the headline in the *L.A. Times*: "Getty Security Guard Saves Ten-Million-Dollar Cézanne." Ten motherfucking million? I had no idea my little friend was so loaded. I'm not crazy about the publicity, what with the stolen identity and all, but I'm sure grateful for the free professional appraisal. I don't even know what to do with that much dough. It might make Mielek more willing to join in the gig, if I can stomach the little psychopath. He did save my ass from getting sliced to death. But first, for once in my life, I gotta figure out how to spend ten grand that I actually earned.

40

Max

The sleeping pills wear off earlier than I hoped, and with them, the sweet amnesia of sleep. As soon as I remember where I am and what happened to Antlop, a deep hole inside me opens up again. I sit in my cell, utterly depleted, dreading the first confrontation since Antlop's murder. It won't be the damaged one delivering food this time. He'll get a talking to. It'll be either the girl or the Teflon guy—or some other bastard. It'll be my turn next, I'm sure. I'm no longer just inconvenient. Now, with the knowledge I have, I've become a dangerous liability.

They're right to be worried. If I'm going to die anyway, I can't let what I know die with me. It's always been my job to bring home the news, even if it's risky. Today is no different. But how could I possibly get this information out? There may not be many more opportunities. I must do it for Antlop, for the hundred plus soldiers and scientists who may have died here, for all of us, for the next generation to learn from our mistakes—if there is a next generation. Only truth has the power to command people's attention and respect, the power to changes minds.

Luckily, it's the Spartan girl who shows up with breakfast—I can tell from her lighter footsteps. She finds me face down on the floor, five pills scattered near my right hand. Wetness pools around my mouth. She's thinking I'm completely out.

"What have you done?" she says.

I don't answer her. I don't even look up. She unlocks the steel gate and kneels at my side. She checks my pulse, my breathing, then turns me over. She's slapping me on the face, my head cradled in her arm, when I finally open my drowsy eyes.

"Oh, it's you," I say, looking at her visor dreamily.

"Why were you saving pills?"

"I thought I'd make your life easier," I say, intentionally slurring my words.

"How many pills did you swallow?" she demands.

"A good number—but obviously not enough." I smile, landing a clumsy hand on her shoulder, then letting it slide down her breast. She must feel my touch through the layers of HazMat fabric.

"You don't even know what I look like." She removes my hand, but doesn't move away.

"Your voice reminds me of my girlfriend's." This time, I place both arms around her waist, slide them down to her hips, her buttocks.

"That's enough." She lets my hands linger on her for a moment more, before peeling them off her hips. "Don't save pills again. You'll suffer."

She helps me back to my cot, forces me to drink some

water, and places the blanket over me. She picks up the stray pills and clicks the gate shut behind her.

When I hear her close the door between the basement and the stairwell, I sit up, alert. I dig into the left sleeve of my jumpsuit and pull out the keycard I'd tucked in there, after extracting it from her hip pocket. Hopefully, it'll take her some time to notice it's missing, because I'm sure she'll make me pay for it. She must have used a different master keycard to unlock the door to the stairwell. Stashing the supposed antidote pills came in handy for a little overdose staging.

Now for the tricky part. I pull out six plastic straws I'd saved from prior meals. With strips of plastic wrap from the food pouches, I bundle up the straws and tie the keycard to one end. It's precarious, but I don't have much else to work with. I stretch my arm as far as I can through the steel bars, holding the clutch of straws as close to the card reader pad as it would go. My fingers are numb from the cold floor. If I drop the card and straws outside my cell and out of reach, it would be the end of me. The straws are not quite long enough to allow the card to make contact with the keypad. With more bits of used plastic wrap, I tie the straws to a piece of cardboard from a tissue box. Again, I extend my arm out as far as I can.

The keycard beeps and the door clicks open for a second. I almost miss it. I get out and try to find my bearings in the darkness, through the labyrinth of black, humming machines with their red and green eyes. Farther away from the brig, I hit upon what looks like the incinerator. A metal cart rests against it, empty, but still coated with human ashes. I look away in disgust. I make for the door to the stairwell, hoping this keycard allows me access to the ground floor.

The heavy door clicks open with a beep. After living so

long in total darkness, my eyes sting in the screaming fluorescent light of the stairwell. I hope the other soldiers are sleeping, recovering from their grisly duties. Sparta is probably still awake though, on guard duty after bringing me breakfast. Who knows how many of them are housed in this building. Breaking into their living quarters is all the excuse they need to finish me off.

The main hallway on the ground floor has the feel of an old, deserted dormitory with linoleum floors. I hear nothing, except a faint sound of heat blowing through the vents. I pass by what look like a series of individual empty laboratory spaces, with lab benches and hooded microscopes. Peeking through the portholes, I don't see any sign of computers. The scientists must supply their own laptops. The labs are too neat, like they hadn't been used all winter. Most of the thousand scientists haven't arrived yet, as the summer season has just begun. There's a red emergency telephone in each lab space, but it probably only calls the local rescue team on call—not much help when I'm escaping from them.

Through the portholes, I stare at the tiny office windows on the opposite side, to get a glimpse of the outside. I miss the pearly daylight, the cleansing air. The sky is white today. Soft snow melting like coconut sorbet. Through these portholes and windows may be the last time I see the world. I try not to dwell on it, and keep moving forward.

The hallways are completely interchangeable. I start paying attention to the room numbers, to avoid going around in circles. At the end of one long hallway, I discover a small, windowless room with no desks at all. It looks like a copier room, with an oversized printer, and what looks like a fax machine. My heart skips. Maybe I can send a fax to Brownell, before they find me. I try my keycard, not sure if it'll open. It actually allows me entry. I close the door behind me slowly, to avoid any noise. It's not clear where my captors are housed, on this floor or another. The clock on the wall tells me I have three more hours until one of them is due to bring me the midday meal. They will see immediately that I'm not in my cell, and initiate a search.

The fax has no dial tone. It requests a passcode. I try standard factory-issued codes like four zeros, 1234. They're rejected. There's nothing else in this room, no phone to the outside, no computer terminal. A dead end. I'm about to head out, when I spot a couple of loose papers on the floor near the fax. They could either be blank sheets or a fax that had fallen off the fax tray, so I decide to flip them over anyway.

It's a fax, sent some three weeks ago, four days after The Day. I hide behind the copier, so no one can see me from the porthole. The font is bold, all caps:

URGENT

TO: ALL MCMURDO RESIDENTS AND STAFF

FROM: US NAVY COMMAND

ATTENTION: REPORT BACK ASAP BY PHONE, FAX, OR EMAIL. We have not heard from you since The Day (October 20th). In light of the complete absence of communication from you following the global amnesia event, we are sending an emergency crew tomorrow, October 25th, 5 p.m. EST. PLEASE ADVISE regarding the situation on the ground. PLEASE INFORM us of any equipment, parts, or medication you need, and what medical, engineering, software or other expertise you require, if any. PLEASE RESPOND ASAP to this communication.

I leaf through the other sheets. It's the same message faxed six times, twice on the first day, and again on four subsequent days. I fold one sheet and stuff it inside my jumpsuit, which has no pockets. There's little doubt now that something happened here, above and beyond the amnesia. My captors are the clean-up crew sent after The Day. Sparta must be a medical doctor. Why did the scientists and staff who had been wintering here fail to communicate back to central command? Or did everyone here die? It makes me shudder.

Why hadn't the US informed the public about a possible accident here? Why the secretiveness? There's only one reason. Something illegal happened here. Not only does the US government not want it known—but they sent a crew to cover it up.

41

Chen

I have high hopes for the first real vacation I can remember. I'm ready to splurge in style after that mother lode bonus. Of course, the trip to Thailand starts out on the wrong foot: the free cocktails on the plane taste like piss on ice. They never give you the alcohol you pay for. Still, I get my money's worth and arrive at the hotel hammered. When I see the hot reception ladies in sarongs, I dream of all the sex I can gorge on in these parts—a small taste of what'll be in store for me once I move here for good.

After the first day, I start having second thoughts about this place though. First, the weather is shit. Why build a city in this muggy, hot hellhole? You can't even walk around the block without sweating like a pig. In this killer heat, I almost faint running after a cab. As for Bangkok traffic, it's L.A. times L.A.—at any hour. The main redeeming quality of this place is the food. I didn't realize there really is such a thing as a culinary orgasm.

As for the sex, that's the second thing I try right off the plane. In a whisper, I ask the concierge for a recommendation, you know, man to man. In front of two middle-aged women waiting in line behind me, the dude pulls out a graphic brochure from a joint called the Tits Café. Boobs flash everywhere as he opens it to the map page. Jeez, there's no modesty in this place. No wonder they call it BangCock. I pocket the brochure and slink away, the two ladies glaring at me like I should have come here for the golden Buddha instead.

∾

At the Tits Café, the two young babes at the counter greet me in unison.

"We have good one just for you."

While I wait, one of them serves me a creamy spiced iced coffee. I drink up while they give the next customer who walks in the same line. Finally, one of them leads me to a tiny room.

Soon a girl shows up, wearing a mini-skirt and a tight t-shirt with a picture of a kitten with this printed underneath: "A$AP PU$$Y." Pile it on, man. The chick is cute and all, but cute as in my little niece who hasn't developed boobies yet. She's way too young to be playing this game. I ask about her age. She giggles and says she can only count to ten in English. That's a very bad sign. Makes me feel like a pedophile, and that's just no good at all. She strips her clothes off, before I can even return the merchandise. No way, José. Naked, she looks like a young teenager. I have fucking limits, man. I leave her a couple of bills, then bolt out of there real fast.

I go stuff myself with an awesome curry instead. After sleeping off the spice, I decide to try again, but with a real woman. I don't want to risk asking the big-mouth concierge again, so I just take a cab to the same Tits Café joint. This time, I ask the girls manning the desk for the oldest they've got, some lady with experience, you know. They act confused, like they simply don't have older women in their country. It's disturbing. I wonder if everybody dies young of AIDS around here. The two gals at the counter whisper to each other. Being the smart business people they are, they say yes anyway, and ask me to sit in the lounge while they scramble to fulfill what they obviously consider to be a weird fetish. They bring me a cold beer and nuts this time. Clearly, I'll be waiting a long time while they go pull some matron out of retirement just for me.

The woman they bring still looks younger than me—but at least she's no kid. She takes things slow, more sensuous and all, like we have all the time in the world. She acts real serious, like we're on some kind of spiritual journey together. She doesn't talk much, maybe because she's the older generation and doesn't know a lick of English. She sure knows the universal language between men and women though. She turns lots of erotic tricks, clever things that feel good in a way that you never even imagined. Not bad, not bad. I'm relaxed and happy all right, and best of all, I don't feel like I'm molesting some kid.

Still, something's not right. Maybe all the heat and humidity is just not good for my constitution, after all the blood I lost fighting with that meth-head at the museum.

The next day, I decide to take it easy in my swanky hotel, chill by the pool or in the air-conditioned lounge, and sip below-freezing Singha beer. But the break from the heat doesn't really do much. Something else is bothering me, and I just can't put my finger on it.

~

That night, after scarfing down another feast of Thai food, I decide to go back to my room and sleep off this never-ending jetlag. Maybe I overdid it with the spices, the heat, the booze, and the sex. In the hotel elevator, I'm stuck with a strange couple. Tall, wrinkly Aussie dude wearing an in-your-face Rolex on one hand, and on the other arm, a young, slinky Asian escort, the type who tries hard to look like potential marriage material just in case the right moron shows up. She's dressed in a beige gown, with an up-do that makes her look like a Chinese Audrey Hepburn if she would just keep her mad teeth out of the picture. Of course, she has to carry a Louis Vuitton bag, like every other waitress, cashier, student, escort, and newlywed here. Only three days in South East Asia, and I already got the message behind the designer bags: "I'm so fucking good in bed that he bought me a three-thousand-dollar piece of cow-skin. What about you?" I mean, for that kinda money, I'd want my own fucking initials printed on the leather.

When the odd pair get off the elevator, I'm disgusted, but I also feel something I haven't felt in a long, long time, at least that I ever remember. I'm feeling lonely, damn it.

Back in my hotel room, I do what I never thought I'd do on this trip: I call Enrika. The surprise phone call from Asia gets her out of her funk and we have a good powwow. I'm really worried about myself after I hang up. There's no more denying that I dig hanging with my cuddly, feisty Enrika more than the quiet, serious dame with the deep bag of sex tricks.

Basically, I can't help wishing that Enrika was here with me too.

42

Max

I must find out more, locate a way to communicate the cover-up to Brownell. As soon as they find out I have Sparta's brig and master keycard, they'll deactivate it. I open the door of the copy room a crack, to make sure the hallway is deserted and silent, then keep walking, peering into each porthole. More unoccupied labs. Then, at the end of the hallway, I come across another small room. This one looks like a windowless janitor's closet. The keycard opens it too.

The trapped air in here smells dank, saturated with chemical cleaning supplies. There are office supplies on a small desk. I stuff a sticky note pad and a pen in my socks, in case they could be useful. Rifling through the desk drawer, I find what looks like a list of room numbers at McMurdo, beside which are columns that indicate whether the room is occupied for the winter, the names of the wintering occupants, and their affiliation. I gasp. About a hundred and twenty people were wintering here. If this list is current, these could be the names of the dead.

Hiding under the desk, in the flickering fluorescent light, I study the names and affiliations of the recent residents. Many are university professors, National Science Foundation grant recipients, and scientists from oceanography institutes. There are two names with the title "US Navy Admin," probably designated officials from the US Navy, which administers McMurdo. I memorize their two room numbers. If anybody knows anything about what happened here, it would be the administrators, especially as it's the Navy that had sent the clean-up crew. One of the administrators is on the floor above this one. I take the list with me.

I listen for any noise, and hearing none, I come out slowly. The stairs are not far from the janitor's closet. The staircase is cold, drafty, and smells of wet cement. I'm shivering in my jumpsuit, which was warm enough in the oppressive dry heat of the basement, but not here.

On the floor above, I emerge in another hallway, this one carpeted. The only sound is of cables swaying in an elevator shaft. One of the administrators' suites is in a far corner of the floor. Of course, there's no porthole on the private residential rooms. I place my ear to the door, but don't hear a sound. Miraculously, the keycard opens it.

This is a nice suite, with a dazzling view of the ice through a small window. I look around to make sure no one is here. There's an outer living space with sofa, TV, kitchenette, a private bathroom, a mini fridge. All I find in the fridge is cans of iced tea. Who the hell would want iced tea in Antarctica? I drink it anyway, if only for the caffeine, and in case I won't find anything else for a while. There must be a computer somewhere here.

The bedroom is almost too neat: bed expertly made, men's leather boots meticulously polished, exercise weights under the bed. Definitely a Navy guy. Nothing looks out of place—which is almost strange in and of itself. On the bedside table is a photograph of a young woman and two girls. I rummage through the desk, the closet, but find nothing of consequence. It's inside a piece of luggage that I spot a sealed Hallmark card, set right atop the neatly packed clothing. It's addressed to "Janet and my Sweeties." I feel bad opening a private note, but I can smell something important:

My beautiful sweetheart, If you're getting this note, then my worst fears have materialized, and it's bad news after all. I can't get into it, but know that I died in the service of our country—and have no regrets. And know that I loved you and cherished you and our beautiful daughters till my last breath.

With love, forever,

Gary

My eyes tear up. Here's this fellow writing a goodbye note before he died. Is he part of the emergency crew—and not expecting to survive the clean-up—or did he die already? I slide my finger on the doorknob of his bathroom. It's dusty. So he hasn't been in here for some time. If he was part of the original gang, which is likely, given that he was on the janitor's list of wintering station managers, then this guy suspected that something was going to happen before it did. Maybe he was instrumental to it, directly or indirectly, and that's why he knew in advance. It's even worse than I thought. It means that what happened here may not have been an accident, after all.

Being in the habit of collecting evidence, I'm about to pocket the guy's card. Then I realize I might not make it out of here alive. This Gary knew how the system works. He knew that this personal effects and card will likely make it back to his wife. So I pull out the Navy's urgent fax and the janitor's list of wintering occupants from my jumpsuit, and insert them into the Hallmark envelope, then reseal it as best I can, and stuff it in one of his jacket pockets. It's insurance, so that Gary's wife will be prompted to ask some questions about what happened here and to whom—in case I can't bring the news safely back home.

After searching the entire suite, I finally find a tablet, deep inside his bedside drawer, in a binder. If this thing is connected, I'll be able to send an email to Brownell. But the tablet also requires a passcode. *Bordel de merde.* I drop the useless thing back in the drawer. I'm running out of time to find some device that's connected.

I take off my jumpsuit, hide it inside the Navy guy's suitcase, and pull some of his clothes on. I'm swimming in them, but at least they keep me warm—and they have big pockets. An idea comes to me when I see the janitor's sticky notes stuffed in my socks. Before I close Gary's suite behind me, I wedge a thick chunk of the sticky note pad in the door jam, to prevent it from locking. This will at least give me somewhere to hide, because sooner or later, they'll deactivate Sparta's keycard, and I'll be stuck out in the hallways, easy prey.

Back in the carpeted corridor, I avoid touching any doors that have no portholes, in case the crew's rooms are on this floor. With all the activity at night, they could still be sleeping in. In the far corner, I find a small room with a porthole—and six TV screens on the wall inside. It looks like an unmanned security room, with surveillance cameras alternating images on the screens. My heart skips. Maybe these could help me locate a business center somewhere in the building, hopefully with a bank of computers for public use, without passcodes on them. I manage to slip in the keycard and gain access. I can't believe my luck.

Inside, it vaguely smells of old food. The garbage bin contains some of those prefabricated meal wrappers, suggesting that the clean-up crew has been here. The camera feeds are alternating on the monitors, but none appear to be recording. Something moves on one of the screens. It's one of the soldiers in HazMat gear, trudging through the slush outside, carrying something. I don't recognize this one's gait, but he has a male stature. The sight of him sends a chill down my back. I steady my nerves, and try to locate a computer. There is none. But there is a regular phone, in addition to the red emergency one. My fingers trembling, I dial Melinda's cell number and wait and pray. But the call to New York doesn't go through. A special code is probably required to call long distance.

I wonder if a call to the French base on Antarctica's coast would perhaps be considered a local call, and therefore require no code. But I have no idea what their number is, if anybody is even there right now. Another soldier pops up on one of the monitors, this time inside an office, looking at a computer screen. The room number that automatically appears at the bottom of the image suggests it's one floor above me. I memorize it, then turn my attention to the surveillance equipment, see if I can understand how it works.

The clean-up crew must have turned off the recording and storing functions soon after they had arrived. Of course: they didn't want any of their cloak and dagger activities on tape. But it looks like they left old footage saved on back-up here—all prior to October 27th—and maybe including recordings of what happened on The Day itself.

43

_____

Max

I immediately scroll around searching for the digital clips from The Day, as that's probably the most informative. There are people everywhere in the screenshots for that October 20th, walking, working, eating, wearing normal clothing inside and out. No one's in HazMat gear. Such a normal day, apparently, that it takes me some time to locate anything eventful.

It first shows up as interference: the images have a shredded quality all of a sudden. Soon after, the people on camera stumble and fall. Of course, we were all losing our balance and getting into accidents that day. But the people on the surveillance videos don't just lose their memories and act confused. They collapse on the floor—and don't move again. I click on random clips between the 20th and the 26th of October. None of the victims get up from where they had fallen. Six days go by without a single person moving on camera—inside or outside the station. They all died—just like that.

What the hell happened here? I focus on the clips right before the interference begins, to see if there's any sign of an explosion right before they all drop. I replay all six camera feeds, but I see nothing, no tremors, no flash in those screenshots that are either outside or in rooms with windows. Some kind of invisible radiation is my first thought. But even radiation doesn't kill instantly unless you're right in ground zero. It's the first time in a while that I crave a cigarette. But there's no time to feel human right now.

I study the earlier clips from The Day. It takes some back and forth to see if there's any unusual activity amongst the many people meandering and working and chatting on the base during what seemed to be an ordinary day. No one was hunkering down, donning any protective gear, or acting fearful or anxious. The only unusual thing I find—about an hour before everybody falls over—is an image from outside the garage. One man—unrecognizable in goggles and hat— takes off in a Skidoo toward Ob Hill. Fifteen minutes later, another man follows him in another Skidoo. Each is carrying a big bag of gear in the rear. I have no idea if this is related to what happens next. They could be going to Ob Hill for research or just for a ride. The only suspicious thing is that the second man looks around him before taking off, as though he's concerned about being seen. A very small gesture in the big scheme of things. It's impossible to tell whether those two Skidoo trips were related to what happened to everybody at the base an hour later.

In his card, Gary confided to his wife that if she receives his farewell letter, his "worst fears have materialized, and it's bad news after all." He didn't share the details, but he told her that he died in the service of his country. I wonder if

Gary had been asked to do something that felt suspicious and risky to him, but was top secret. The type of request that comes not from his direct superiors at the Navy, but from high up in the echelons of power. It's more like the kind of thing the Pentagon would do.

I fast forward to the 27th to understand what happened right after the clean-up crew arrived, and just before they cut off the recordings. But before I get to it, a loud alarm goes off from the ceiling. It jolts me right to the bone. Could it be a fire alarm? Through the porthole, I look out into the hallway, but see nothing.

Just then, a voice blurts out from a loudspeaker:

"Attention, Attention, all staff. Fugitive on the loose. Fugitive on the loose. Max Cattelain, it is in your best interests to turn yourself in now. Attention all staff. Fugitive could be armed and dangerous. Orders to capture dead or alive. Repeat. Fugitive could be armed and dangerous. Orders to neutralize on sight."

My heart pumps with adrenaline. I'm at my wits' end. They're after me again, before I was able to relay any information to the outside world. I need to get out of this room immediately. They'll surely come in here soon to look at the cameras and locate where I am. I open the door and run for it.

44

Chen

Back from Bangkok, I find bad news waiting for me. While I was gone, my lovely pomegranates got a new frame, this one with Plexiglass. Now they're armed to the hilt too. It figures, after the spineless attack that almost killed the painting. What the hell am I gonna do now? It leaves me crabby all day.

"After all that Asian sex, you come back depressed?" Mielek smirks.

"It's a downer when the party's over," I say, thinking of the painting, not the Thai chicks. Good thing I never did try to recruit Mielek. Now, who's kidding who, after all that sweat, the artwork gig doesn't look too good no more. I'd be suicidal to go ahead with it.

The only good thing I come back home to is Enrika, though she's still mad that I didn't take her on a romantic vacation instead. At least the pricy phone calls from Asia proved that I was thinking about her. The sexy sarongs I brought her help things along too. Problem is, after my trip, she's one horny bitch, camping at my place all week long, trying to make up for lost time. I have a hard time keeping up with her, after all the overtime my poor cock was doing over there.

Soon, Enrika spends so much time at my place that I find her cafeteria uniform hanging in my closet, her glow-in-the-dark lingerie in my drawer, and her taco wares in my kitchenette. The sex finally slows down and we watch way too many movies together. She starts wearing sweat pants around the apartment. She even invites her four brothers over to watch a soccer game one Sunday after their lousy TV broke down. It's a little too much intimacy, if you ask me. If she's not careful, she'll go from being a sex kitten to a fat cat who sleeps in the same hairy patch on the couch. At least her four brothers agree to a round of poker, so I can squeeze some hard-earned greenbacks from them.

Secretly, I torment myself about when the time will come to vacate for good. Now that the baby Cézanne is out of reach, what's my next step? Maybe I can find another small piece that's unarmed and valuable. Or maybe I go back to Thailand and try to open a shady business with what's left of my ten grand. It would last me a year—then what? All this puts me in a funk.

I tell Enrika to renew her passport, so that she'll be on board for the next vacation abroad. She laughs like it's the biggest joke, 'cause she's been illegal since she was a baby and crossed the desert on all fours. She's not going anywhere outside the US of A, she says, 'cause they'd never let her come back. Besides, I know she'd miss her family— and they'd come looking for her, hedge trimmers in hand.

45

Max

The loud alarm goes off again, jangling my nerves. The same announcement rattles off over the PA system, effectively giving all of them license to kill me—when I'm neither armed nor dangerous. It'll be impossible to hear footsteps in the hallway with this racket. I try to duck into a private residential room. Soon enough, they'll realize I have Sparta's master key, and promptly deactivate it.

There's no alternative but to go back to the US Navy administrator's suite, and hope that the door I'd propped open didn't close shut. I'm retracing my steps to the opposite side of the floor, when I hear the unmistakable barking of a police dog.

Great. I remember reading somewhere that dogs—and any non-human species of any kind—are no longer allowed on Antarctica. Chances are they've been transgressing even more important parts of the 1959 Treaty, so what's a canine?

The barking continues, strident, but I can tell it's farther away, muffled. Maybe they're in the staircase. The police dog was probably brought here to sniff out corpses in the buildings and in the snow. I try to convince myself that as long as I'm still alive, my scent is not what the canine is trained to sniff out.

The dog barks again somewhere in the bowels of the building. I need to get out of here and find a way to reach Brownell.

Someone must be manning the cameras now. It's best to leave this floor, so I don't unexpectedly run into anybody going in or out of the surveillance room. Listening for sounds, I climb up another set of stairs. Halfway down another long corridor, I locate what looks like a big communal office, with a dazzling view of the expanse of ice and of Ob Hill. So the communal areas are up here to take advantage of the view. Through the porthole, rows and rows of computers sit idle and dark. My spirits lift. This is what I need. This is my one chance. I must find a way to get in here. But as much as I try, I can't gain entry with my disabled keycard anymore. Why didn't I come here first, damn it? I shake the doorknob. I'm hovering on the edge of despair. Soon they'll know where I am, because they'll be monitoring which doors I tried—and failed—to open with this keycard. They'll find me—and I'll be dealt the same fate as Antlop.

I turn away from the door. I force myself to be optimistic. Not my forte.

An elevator makes that little gay sound when it arrives at the requested floor. I round the corner. Bulky footsteps echo on the hardwoods. This could be the floor where they're camping. I wait till a door opens and closes, then I forge ahead while I can. I peer into the porthole of a double door. This one is the kitchen, what they call the galley here, clearly underutilized now that they're only consuming prepackaged emergency food. I'm about to move on, but decide to try the door anyway, if only to look for a sharp object that I can use as a weapon if I have to. Surprisingly, it opens. Maybe the heavy steel door was left unlocked for safety reasons: in case the entire keycard system malfunctions, residents wouldn't be denied access to food.

The steel countertops, industrial stove, and all surfaces in between are covered with a sticky dust. A narrow, but deep pantry to the side of the kitchen is still filled to the brim with canned goods, dry pasta, and cooking oil. In the cramped space, I move carefully to avoid dropping anything that would make noise. If I do find a knife or scissors, all I'll be doing is helping them justify killing me on sight. Just then my eyes land on a narrow desk built into the shelving of the pantry. Concealed by a stack of cookbooks and recipe binders is a small PC laptop, probably for storing recipes and ordering supplies on the next plane. My fingers tremble with excitement and dread, as I try to turn it on.

It makes a loud jingle. Just what I needed. I put it on mute. To my utter amazement, the McMurdo home page flicks on, no password required. That means it's hooked to the station's internet. I look for a door to close behind me, but the pantry has no door.

It's not clear if I can access external websites or at least Skype. I type in the *New York Times* website and wait. It's awfully slow. I look up to see if anybody is watching me through the double-door porthole. No one. The *New York Times* home page appears, familiar and comforting. In utter disbelief, I begin writing an email to Brownell. This is my one chance.

My stiff, cold fingers trip on the keyboard as I inform him of the Navy's urgent fax, and the subsequent arrival of a clean-up crew on October 27th, after surveillance cameras had recorded everyone at the station dropping dead all at once on The Day. I tell him how the fatalities most likely included all those wintering at McMurdo, which, according to a janitor's occupancy list, run well over a hundred people. I describe the clean-up crew's secretiveness, hostility, Level A HazMat suits, and their nightmarish directive to find, incinerate, and apparently destroy evidence of those who died at the base. I mention the personal farewell card I found in the luggage of one of two US Navy station managers, suggesting that he had advance knowledge of something that could threaten his life, something that he considered part of his service to the country.

I note how just prior to the event, surveillance cameras showed just another day at the station, where nobody was wearing protective gear or hiding in bunkers, suggesting that most scientists and staff did not appear to know that a planned and imminent event could kill them. I conclude that I have no idea what they were up to, but that there were two men on camera who took Skidoos to Ob Hill an hour before the event, carrying bulky gear.

I tell Brownell that I don't know the nature of the event, if it was a bona fide science experiment or something that could be construed as illegal under 1959 Treaty rules. All I know is that two people who looked like they were hiding something drove up in the direction of Ob Hill, an hour before all the residents dropped dead instantly, on the Day. I add that the Amundsen-Scott base seems to be completely unaware of anything odd going on at McMurdo, and flights between both bases are cancelled.

I weave in our own 911 emergency call data that show the earliest amnesia-related calls started in the southern tip of Australia and the latest calls were way up in the Northern hemisphere. This is consistent with the possibility that McMurdo was the epicenter. I end by documenting Antlop's unjust death.

Typing up the piece calms me, gives a modicum of meaning to my existence—what's left of it. For a moment, I lose myself in the clean and orderly realm of the word, so oblivious to the senseless and violent world around me that I fail to notice anything else. Especially not someone entering the galley.

The first thing I hear is the rustling of synthetic fabric. I know that sickening sound all too well now. I instinctively rest my fingertips on the keyboard and look up. An ugly figure in a HazMat suit. From her height, I can tell it's her. She's aiming a gun at me. My heart jolts.

"Hands up," she says.

I force myself not to obey.

"You heard me. I'll shoot if you hit send," she says.

Her tone tells me she's miffed, that she knows my moves and feigned overdose were a set up. What she doesn't know is that I'd rather die quickly with one final victory, than slowly and futilely. My eyes still on her, and without looking at the keyboard, I type the shortcut "Alt s" to send the email.

She fires at me, three deafening shots that blast through everything.

46

Max

When I open my eyes, my ears are still ringing from the gunshots, my hands trembling. I don't feel pain, but I know I can't trust that. I inspect my limbs, my trunk. The bullets didn't go through my body. Instead, Sparta aimed for the laptop, which is smoldering now, three clean shots through the keyboard, straight through the desk, the linoleum. As I'm making sense of what happened, the Spartan girl shoves me away from the smoking computer to determine whether the email went through. What is faster, internet or bullet? All I know is the bullet always wins.

"Why did you do this to us? Why?" It's the first time I hear any kind of emotion in her voice.

She stares me down from behind her dark visor, demanding an answer, her gun jammed against my ribs now. She's acting like I did this to destroy her personally.

"I didn't do this to hurt you," I say, trying to calm my voice, to be very still, hoping she doesn't shoot me. "People need to know. And it's not fair to you to do the dirty work of hiding it."

Still aiming the gun at me, I can tell she's seething, weighing the ramifications of each decision, depending on whether the email went through: to shoot or not to shoot the journalist. If the email was not delivered, it would be acceptable to kill me—after all, I had escaped my cell and penetrated their living quarters, and could have placed their lives in danger. If the email went through, however, shooting me at point-blank wouldn't be a wise decision. Finally, she walks away from me in silence.

Three soldiers rush into the galley. Sparta makes a gesture toward me, and the even-keeled one handcuffs me. Another soldier starts dousing the smoldering plastic and linoleum with a fire extinguisher. So there are a few other people at the station.

Sparta turns to the angry, broken soldier. "Take him out," she says, lifting a gloved palm in the air in my general direction, like she's shooing a fly away.

Shit, maybe I underestimated her. I bite my lip.

The nasty one pats me down, then takes me back to the basement.

"Why did you do that?" he says on the way down to the mechanical underworld I hoped never to see again. "We don't need this." He shakes his head.

The soldier takes a turn into an unfamiliar hallway, stacked with rusting snowplowing equipment. He opens a heavy metal door. I recognize its particularly high-pitched creaking. It's the door to the outside.

"There you go, you got your freedom now," he says.

I wish freedom were as pure as the word. A gush of frigid wind slams into my face—and I'm only at the threshold.

He's not shoving me out, but just waiting for me to walk to my own death.

"You really need to stuff one more body in the incinerator?" I say.

"I'm just following orders," he says, looking down.

"Yep, we know how that ends," I say.

He says nothing.

"Look, I'm going to die anyway, so at least tell me who I have to thank for it," I say.

"Why don't you just figure it out for yourself? You tell me, who creates this kind of mess, then has other people clean it up?"

I know the soldier is obviously resentful at all the shitty orders coming from above, including this.

"The Pentagon," I say softly.

"Damn right," he says, surprised by my quick response. I say nothing and stay still, hoping he keeps talking. He looks behind his shoulder, to see if there's anybody around. "They sent them some fucking experiment to do in minus forty, without telling them what the hell it was. They didn't even tell people to put on some gear." And then he stops. He already said too much, carried away by his black anger, by the ghostly faces of the corpses, perhaps by frozen body parts dropping on the concrete and chipping off like icicles —because that's what it sounded like that night when Sparta said she had a broken bag.

He looks down at the snow, remembering. This is his way of rebelling, a small way to preserve what's left of his humanity.

"It was supposed to be a few muons—super muons, who knows what they did to them."

How strange, I remember what I know about muons: cosmic particles that pass through everything all the time, through our bodies, right through the whole planet. Never hurt a thing. Totally inert. I say nothing.

"Next thing you know, they all drop dead."

I can't believe what he just told me. The soldier laid out what could be a causal relationship between the doomed super muon experiment and the collective amnesia, because the folks here all died on The Day, and the amnesia spread from the South Pole everywhere else.

He doesn't say anything more. He's said it all.

"Thanks," I say, nodding. I force myself to make his job easier: I start walking through the door, into the frosty wind, towards my last hours on this earth.

"Sorry, man," he says, as he closes the metal door shut behind him.

It's one of those white days, when the sky and snow are melded into one. The sun forms a ghostly presence behind the smoky clouds. After so much gloom, the white light burns holes in my eyes. The wind whirls fresh snow on my cheeks. It feels good to be outside after so long in that dark, suffocating death chamber, where I was inhaling human dust.

I am surprisingly more at peace after what the soldier told me. He turned out to be the most humane one, after all. There is deliverance in the truth.

So they were testing some new weapon, the bastards, against treaty rules. They took inert muons and weaponized them. It's so much more clear to me now. Muons are everywhere, particles that penetrate everything in the cosmos and come out the other side. There's no way to contain them, because they go through lead, concrete, through the crust and core of our entire globe. They travel great distances across the universe at essentially the speed of light, so nothing can stop them.

The weapon only killed the scientists here because they were so close. But for the rest of us, the muons spreading all over the planet—from South to North—only affected our memory. When these super muons go through the human skull, they must damage the most sensitive part of the brain —the hippocampus and its autobiographical memory stores —and go right back out, without visibly disturbing any other tissue, leaving no trace.

The Navy guys were probably told it's nothing at all— just inert muons, a little more excitable than usual. But the new, doctored particles went right through Ob Hill and killed everyone on the spot.

As if nukes aren't enough, they needed to develop a weapon that robs people of their memories, their identity, the very reason they're fighting—even their will to fight. It keeps victims alive but reduces them to sheep. It's an unconscionable, unjust weapon of war. Imagine if the survivors of Hiroshima and Nagasaki were also robbed of their identity, the memories of those who perished—and the knowledge of who had dropped the bombs.

I just wish I knew all of this when I still had access to email. Now, this secret will die with me. That's just too bad.

My entire body is shivering now, my teeth clattering. I could pretend to take a long walk in the snow, knowing that in a matter of hours my freedom will become my demise. Very soon it'll be painful out here, with no coat, no gloves, and my hands handcuffed behind my back with cold metal. The memory of Antlop's metallic grating leaves me shuddering. In the moments before it becomes impossible, I admire the tender snow that has fallen so equally over everything.

47

Chen

As senior guard now, I'm the last one to clock out Tuesdays and Thursdays. There are always stragglers to herd out. They're usually dreamy, nostalgic types, who look at the art like it holds answers to life's mysteries. I mean, don't you have homes to go to? Besides, it's raining tonight. You'd think they'd want to give themselves some extra time on the road since California drivers lose their balls when it drizzles.

After the last patrons finally clear out, I take one last lookie-look, make sure no kid or grandma has been left behind. Next thing I know, the lights go out. Just like that. Figures, the second it rains in L.A., the whole shoddy infrastructure falls apart.

At first, I'm miffed that it's pitch black and I don't have my flashlight on me. Then I realize what this means: my Cézanne is unarmed and the cameras can't see shit. These were the only two big hurdles left to finishing the job. And the doors are wide open as we haven't closed up just yet.

Wait, that's too good to be true. I listen to see if the back-up diesel generator kicked in already. Nothing. With all the confusion, they might have forgotten to test it.

I hustle to the Impressionist galleries, the battery-powered exit signs in the hallways giving out just enough light. By now, I can walk this place in the dark.

There's my beauty, ready for the taking. I run my fingers around the frame, barely touching her. My heart flutters. I can't believe it. I couldn't have planned it better than this. Still no sound of the diesel generator.

There is one small hiccup though. I have no idea how long this blackout is gonna last. It can be a day, an hour, or just one more minute.

I'm feeling lucky, though. This is the miracle I've been waiting for the entire time. I take a solid breath. My palms sweating, my fingers trembling, I remove her from the hook, ever so gently.

She doesn't make a peep: the alarm is dead—for now. The gaudy frame is heavier than it looks. That was the hardest part, the part that was a deal-breaker. With the cameras blind and the doors unarmed, the rest of my exit out of the museum should be easy now—as long as I have a little time. I'd timed it many times: I need exactly twelve minutes flat to run down the hill and get out onto the street and into my car.

The heavy painting in my hands, I mentally run through the steps I'd memorized down pat: first, I'd place her in the oversized sports backpack in my locker; then I'd run out the emergency exit off the cafeteria, which puts me closest to the street. I always park my car on the street, far from any cameras, so I can just walk normally to my car, then skedaddle. Next, I'd buy a ticket to Jakarta for tonight, using my real passport, since the museum doesn't know me as Alec Chen. There's gotta be a hundred Chens going to Asia. For at least a day or two, they wouldn't suspect me, 'cause I saved the same painting from that punk. By that time, there'll be no trace of Maxi-Million left on U.S. soil—except maybe some dude getting high in an alley.

In the morning, L.A. time, I'd find an internet café in Jakarta and call in sick with the flu, so management wouldn't suspect me right away. Once in Asia, again under my Asian name, I'd buy a separate ticket to Bangkok through some other carrier. Then I'd kiss the Getty goodbye.

48

Max

All too soon, my breath clouds over. My throat and lungs start stinging in the subzero temperatures. In the wind, my tears feel like razor blades down my cheeks. My fingers and ears are the first to suffer. Every muscle in my body twitches uncontrollably. Walking is not enough to stay warm. I try running, but it's too awkward with my hands handcuffed behind my back. I start jumping in place, trying to generate heat. The surge of warmth expanding through my body gives me some hope. Maybe they're only punishing me. Maybe they'll come back for me.

Another bout of jumping to keep up the temperature. Then the inevitable slip on the ice. My face and knees slam into ice-covered concrete. Pain shoots through my bad knee. With my hands tied, each time I try to get up, I slip again. The icy slush soaks through my clothes and steals any heat I have left. They're not just teaching me a lesson; they're making me pay.

Who knows if my email actually went through. The sad thing is I had enough time to send the email to Brownell if I had written it as a telegram, in four sentences flat. They come so easily to me now, like a haiku. Instead, I had to write a whole fucking article, with perfect grammar. I'm a perfectionistic prick and look where that got me.

As for the soldiers, they're in big trouble as it is. Yet another casualty, another body won't make a difference. After all, if their orders were "kill on sight," that covers all outcomes.

I've now exhausted everything I have left in me. I don't want to fight for survival anymore. I'm done with hope. Drenched in ice-cold water, walking on my knees in the snow, I finally make it back behind the metal door, where at least there's shelter from the wind. That must be why Antlop remained there till the end. It's much easier to stay right here and stop moving. Every time I move, the ice-cold metal of my hand-cuffs sticks to another part of my hands, ripping out the skin. Unlike Antlop, I know that asking for help, yelling, and scratching is futile. I save my breath to relish the last thoughts I will ever have.

I've probably had many moments like this in my life as a war correspondent, the most recent—and memorable—in Syria. What do people do in these last minutes of lucidity? Ideally, I'd think about the meaning of my life, or conjure up one last time all the people I loved. Sadly, the amnesia has taken all that away from me. I don't remember the meaning of my life, if there ever was one. Could it really have been to witness and document human decrepitude? Sometimes I'm convinced that reporting on evil actually normalizes it, glamorizes it, even inspires others to try it.

Maybe we're better off saving the front page for acts of altruism.

Thinking of my loved ones one last time is not possible, given that I've forgotten them all. It's the first time I feel cheated of my past. My minutes are running out. My blood will freeze over soon. This will be the complete, the permanent amnesia, the one from which there is no waking, the one place where memories can't follow. I'm ready for it too.

Then I remember the one positive memory I've formed since The Day.

I think of the universes in Rani's eyes; the warmth of her breasts under her fuzzy sweater; and her passionate kisses, each like a drop of fire. She feels light years away from me now, like a planet I'll never visit in my lifetime.

49

Chen

I've been lost in thought, frozen here, going through the plan in my head, the frame weighing me down. What the hell are you waiting for, dude? Time is ticking, damn it. The electricity can go back on any minute now. The painting alarm will sound; the lights will go back on; and the camera will record you with the Cézanne in your hands. Get the fuck out of here, Chen.

I think of Enrika one last time. She'll scream every Spanish curse she knows at a hundred miles an hour. This loaded beauty in my hands is my real mistress, what I came here for. Come on, Chen, shit or get off the pot. Every minute can cost you a decade behind bars.

And what if I get caught? I don't wanna spend the rest of my life in a shithole prison.

Make a fucking decision, Chen. Take the bloody pome-granates or not. Scram and risk jail time—or live this weird middle class life like you're Joe Normal. Never see Enrika again or stay and give her a baby. Keep earning a living or snatch it once and for all.

A heavy fatigue falls over me. I'm feeling funny. Something's changed, something that I'm pretty sure wasn't there before. It feels like I have more options, like I have more to lose now, 'cause my life isn't so bad anymore. Why risk the lock-up for a bunch of underage Thai chicks who're turning tricks for chewing gum money?

I don't know what the hell is wrong with me. My sweaty hands start lifting the gilded frame toward the wall again. Look at you, Chen, flip-flopping all over the place. With one last hoist, I set it back on its hooks.

You lost your touch, man. Such a sweet opportunity totally wasted on you. You're not a pro, but just a lowly pick-pocket. Ten million dollars down the toilet. Now you're gonna earn peanuts clocking in at twenty bucks an hour for the rest of your life.

I'm still berating myself, feeling like shit, staring at my beauty on the wall when the lights snap back on. I almost faint.

I look at my watch. There was no way I would've had enough time in four minutes to make it out to the street, away from the cameras. I would have been caught on camera near the gates. I can't believe it: my dilly-dallying actually saved my ass.

The cameras must be back on too now. I force myself to move away from the painting. I walk out of the gallery, slowly, trying not to shake. I make a point of looking into every room and checking on every piece along the way, steady, back to security guard mode for the benefit of the camera boys. But inside, it feels like I'm racing down the highest roller coaster.

I know then that I could never steal another thing in my life.

You know what this means, Chen? It means you've got no other choice but to hang onto this job and this girl, and kiss the ground that you're still a free man.

50

Max

It's impossible to say how much time has gone by. Long enough to be overwhelmed by the cold, numb to its destruction of tissue. I must have temporarily lost consciousness—a bad sign. I can no longer think of anything but death. Here I am, dying alone. That's how we all die, anyway. Soon, I'll become part of the inert world and these things won't matter to me anymore.

Something flickers in the whiteness. It looks denser than the fresh snow blowing off the ground, white against white. I squint in the glare, trying to make out if it's a mirage or a person.

Then I see the dark visor. One of them is coming to finish me off. I should have died already. I lasted too long, and now I'm blocking the doorway, preventing them from wheeling in more bodies from outside. It's just as well. I'm too tired, and everything hurts. I try to gauge who it is by height or gait, but in my state, I can't measure anything against the shifting white background. In silence, the figure hovers at close range and stops to pull something out of a hip pocket. I close my eyes and wait for a gunshot, feeling more relief than dread.

The beep of a keycard reader confuses me, followed by the creaking of the metal door. I open my eyes, perplexed. Then the figure drags me inside by the armpits, back into the dark underbelly of McMurdo, all the way back to my cell. I did not expect this of all things.

"You'd better not tell them I said anything," says the same soldier who'd put me out in the snow.

"OK," I manage to utter through frozen lips.

He throws a blanket over me before slamming the iron gate shut.

The broken soldier returns with a meal and hot tea. With my numb fingers, I barely manage to take a few sips of tea before it spills. I leave the food untouched. I shiver under the blanket, in and out of consciousness, before sleep claims over my cold body. I can't move, can't stay awake, and can't warm up. It's over. My body can no longer change course.

A loud sound catapults me from my slumber. The first thing I think of is the incinerator, because that's always the horrid sound in my nightmares. Will they put me in there alive? Despair fills every corner of my mind. Dying is one thing, but being burnt alive is a whole different story. I sit up and listen carefully, my heart beating erratically. This one is a continuous sound. It's coming from the outside, far away, a sound I haven't heard since I came here. It's the motor of an LC-130 floating overhead, preparing to land on the

McMurdo airstrip. I hope it's a good thing, but I find hope just too exhausting right now.

For what feels like several excruciating hours, I strain my ears—but nothing changes. How naïve I am. It's probably just a routine delivery of goods. I close my eyes once more and let my body descend into hibernation, into oblivion.

51

Max

What feels like hours later, loud footsteps wake me up again. I open my leaden eyes and see all three soldiers standing stiff in their protective gear, facing my cell. It's easy to recognize them when I can compare their heights. This can only be bad news. All I can think of is death by firing squad.

"He's here." It's Sparta's resentful voice.

Another set of footsteps approaches. A new person has arrived, perhaps a higher-up. I dread what else they have in store for me. I expect a faceless general in a HazMat suit.

Instead, standing outside my cell I see a man in a perfectly tailored Yves Saint Laurent cashmere coat, with kid gloves matching the lapels.

"Time to go back home, *mon cher* Max," says Jeffrey Brownell in his underwater voice and his only two words of French.

·   ·   ·

While the chartered plane is refueling, Brownell wraps me in a down sleeping bag, and bandages my frostbitten fingertips as best he can. He feeds me hot instant soup, since my fingers are worthless. He's surprisingly good at his nursing duties. I'm still too far gone to talk, drifting into sleep as soon as I'm left to my own devices. So he takes it upon himself to keep the chatter going, just to keep me awake.

After takeoff, there's relief written all over his face. It must not have been easy to negotiate my release with the top brass. Against all odds, the internet whisked away my email right before Sparta shot the laptop, thanks to the keyboard shortcut I had used. Brownell published my piece immediately on the website, then in that morning's paper.

"I wish you were there when I got your email," he said, grinning. "Not one editor wanted to change a thing. They didn't even want to correct the two typos. It was like this sacred text had just fallen from the sky and landed on the printing press."

When Brownell called the Department of Defense to secure my release, a General Kelty informed him that I'd attempted an escape and died of hypothermia.

"I told him I just don't believe it," says Brownell, "because Cattelain hates the cold, and besides, he has other preferred methods of killing himself. So I told him to retract the escape bullshit before I publish it too, and drag him personally into the scandal."

This makes me smile.

"Since they couldn't kill the messenger, they decided to charge you with attempting to break into a government installation for purposes of military espionage," says Brownell. "I told him it's hardly military espionage when a reporter shows up to a research installation that's supposed to be for scientific purposes only—and then stumbles on military secrets that have no business being there. Anyway, they're the ones on trial right now, not you. They've got a lot of explaining to do. Everyone is convinced this is no accident, that they were experimenting with something, against treaty rules. Even the US Navy is pissed, because the Pentagon used their guys on the ground, without the higher-ups being told anything about it—until they were asked to clean it up."

"The soldier told me what they were testing," I say, even though talking is still hard. "He thought I was gonna die."

"What? What did he tell you?" asks Brownell.

I tell him about the super muons they had tested, clearly without a good understanding of the ramifications.

"What bastards," says Brownell. Then he smells the fresh scent of breaking news. "This is gonna be sweet," he says. "Look what's happening already."

Brownell powers up his laptop and shows me a snapshot of the news frenzy sparked by my article. Protests erupted in cities all over the globe. Predictably, people are demanding an investigation into the cover-up, and an explanation as to what lethal experiment or accident could have caused the deaths—and whether this is what caused the global amnesia.

"Look what you've accomplished, Max, something that journalists have long stopped dreaming of," Brownell says.

I remember the Op-Ed I'd read on the icy road to McMurdo. For once, we're all outraged at the same time, because we all lost the same thing. Maybe we might actually do something about it. It is indeed a lot more than I ever dreamed of.

52

Max

When I finally walk into my apartment a few days later, I find a powdery white layer coating every surface. Dust particles dance in the wall of sunshine, like uncanny snowflakes.

With bandaged fingers, I yank the rest of the shades up and thrust open the windows. In my hurry to meet Brownell in New York, I had neglected to prepare my apartment for a long absence. Food is rotting in the fridge. I take out the stinky garbage and wash a load of laundry on the hottest setting. Digging around the old backpack that Brownell had managed to retrieve from my captors, I find the methadone pills. I toss them. I don't need them anymore and I don't want to keep them around. There's a stash of old crumpled newspapers in there too. As I'm stuffing them in the recycling bin, the manila envelope falls out. After Antlop had opened it, the tape never stuck back in place, and Sylvia's scratchy cursive is naked, in the open, tormenting me. The notes are now a painful reminder of Antlop too. I stare at them frozen, not knowing what to do.

I remind myself that I don't have to do anything. Maybe I'll just stick them in my vest pocket, where they used to be. It feels like not much has changed in my life. I'm really just going around in circles. Back in my apartment, that old emptiness descends on me again. In the shower, I place my head under scalding water, hoping it will burn off the nonsense gripping me.

I craved my own bed and my own space the entire time in captivity. But now my seven hundred square feet of solitude suffocate me more than my cell in McMurdo.

I put on wool socks, my warmest cashmere sweater, my vest, then get out of this place. After picking up the paper, I walk to the nearest café in Santa Monica. While I wait for my coffee, I bury myself in the *L.A. Times*. I'm hoping the motions of normality will somehow restore it, but I have my doubts. Start with the uplifting news, I tell myself.

There's a flurry of articles that tag onto our story about the super muons. Protests are erupting everywhere, not only in the US, but in other nuclear-club countries: Russia, France, Great Britain, China, India, and Pakistan. Millions of citizens all over the world are also questioning their own governments' continued research into new and better ways to destroy ourselves. I inspect the photograph of a protester sitting in front of the Pentagon, holding up a poster: "This time we lost our past. Next time, we lose our future."

Citizens all over the world are organizing to pressure their governments to denuclearize—and to stop developing unethical weapons of war, in the aftermath of the McMurdo cover-up. That at least makes me smile.

I turn to the L.A. news section. On the local front, there's an article about a security guard at the Getty who was hailed a hero. He guarded the entire collection during a long black-out when the alarms were disabled and the doors were wide open. The same guy had previously saved a Cézanne from being defiled. What? He has my same name! Maybe this is why the gatekeeper in Antarctica had seen the Getty listed as my employer in my credit history. Perhaps she made a mistake because we have the same name. But she was using my own social security number to pull up the report. That makes no sense. For all I know, we're related. Might be worth paying this Maximilien a visit. Not that I have anything else more pressing to do. I grab a cab to the Getty.

53

Max

At the information desk, I'm told this guy works in the main building of the museum. Once there, I ask the first guard I see where to find Maximilien Cattelain.

"Ah, that's how it's pronounced," he says with a thick Eastern European accent. He's a big, solid, timber-chopping kind of guy with a creepy smirk that looks more like a wince. "How do you know Frenchie?" he says.

The guy's nickname catches me by surprise. He must be French too.

"I'm a journalist for The New York Times," I say. "I saw the article in the local paper, and wanted to interview him for a longer piece."

He rolls his eyes at the sickening adulation of his colleague, then brings a walkie-talkie to his bluish lips.

"Hey, Frenchie, you've got a visitor."

When this famous security guard shows up, I do a double take. He's Asian—and doesn't sound French at all.

He has a rough American accent that says born and raised on the street. He walks with a swagger, like he had to look dangerous just to survive till the next birthday. Short, compact, looking put together in the security guard uniform. I ask him for an interview, so we can at least sit for a chat.

"That's nice of you and all, but I'm real shy, you know," he says, eyes shifty. I know then that he's hiding something. "I don't really like all this attention on me," he adds.

"I insist," I say. "There's something else I want to talk to you about, something that you and I have in common," I whisper, my eye on the Eastern European guard hovering nearby, shamelessly eavesdropping.

A small panic ripples through Frenchie's eyes.

"Let's go have a bite to eat," he says. "Mielek, clock me out for a late lunch, and cover for me, will you?"

"Sure," says the giant guard, still smirking. "You're coming back, right?"

"Very funny—no, I be gone forever," says Frenchie.

He leads me away toward the exit of the museum.

"I thought we're meeting around here?" I say, pointing to the museum cafeteria.

"Nah. Food's all right in there, but the cafeteria chicks will wanna fatten you up like a Christmas goose, especially with your bandaged fingers and all. What happened to you, anyway? You got into a fight or something?"

"You can say that." It makes me nervous to follow this guy I don't know off the premises, but he is a security guard. He claims there's a bar right down the street that's open all day long. It's a nice neighborhood, but the car culture means there's hardly anybody walking these sidewalks.

"Least I can do is buy you a beer, man," he tells me. "That Mielek is a human video-camera. We don't wanna be talking anywhere near him."

We duck into the classic dark, seedy bar, the last place left in America where a guy is allowed to be a caveman, burp, get sloppy drunk, and start a fight if he wants to, any day, any hour. Neon signs advertise beer brands that are long gone. The old carpet flaunts its biggest stains in defiance. The stuffy air smells of stale fries, hamburger patties gone cold, and upholstery that's never been laundered. There's a steady clientele of weather-beaten laborers sitting next to pasty loafers and hangers-on, some too hairy, some very old, but all with a gripe to nurse. The older waitress has a "I can't believe I'm still working here" look on her face. She mechanically sprinkles her speech with enough 'sweeties' and 'honeys' to exact a kinder tip. Her oversized cleavage has seen better days, but her wardrobe M.O. hasn't changed: show off what you've got and hope for the best.

Frenchie glances at my vest, now a bit too loose on my shoulders.

"Get him the biggest burger you've got," he tells the waitress. "And extra onion rings."

I tell him I'm not hungry, but he ignores me.

"My treat. And four pints of whatever's on draft to save time," he tells her, then turns back to me. "So you really a journalist?"

"Yep."

"Not a cop?"

"Not a cop." This is a bad start.

"So what's the thing we have in common?" he says.

"My name."

He huffs out a long breath through pursed lips like he burnt his fingers on something.

"You Maxi-million Cattelain?"

He makes my name sound like some stupid game show. I know then there's no way it's his real name.

"That's right. Where did you get my name from?" I say.

He doesn't admit or deny anything, and the waitress conveniently saves him, by placing four cold ones on the table. He takes a few noisy gulps of beer, biding time.

"You didn't find my lost driver's license somewhere by any chance?" I ask.

"All right, all right. Listen up, I'll come clean, but you gotta give a man a break."

"I'm listening."

He finishes the first pint like it's a glass of water in the desert. The waitress brings a greasy fat cheeseburger and oversized golden onion rings.

"These are some of the best in town, you know." He munches on the biggest one before he begins. "All right, here's the God-honest truth. I saved your life, man. You were left for dead, and I called 911 when this cashier broad was gonna let you croak just because she was 'busy with customa.'" He says this last bit with a Taiwanese accent. "And I'm no friend of the police, you know. I don't like chatting it up with those guys."

This is a complete surprise. Could he really be the good Samaritan that the ER doc mentioned?

"What?" I mutter.

"Yeah, thanks for the thank you note you didn't send. You're the guy who almost OD'ed in the alley behind the Seven Eleven on Santa Monica Boulevard—that's what."

He's got the right alley, and the correct diagnosis. He must be telling the truth. I don't even know what to say. I feel bad that I've been gruff with him.

"Thanks, man." I shake his hand.

"Good luck finding another Chen to save your hide next time."

"Your real name is Chen?"

He sighs, realizing he slipped.

"Yeah. Alec Chen. Call me Chen. Miss my name too.

Easy to pronounce and easy to spell."

"I could see that. I owe you one, Chen."

"Well, here's the thing. You owe me one—but let's just say you've already returned the favor. See, I felt lousy, but I thought you were dead or on your way there, anyways. Besides, I had no choice. I needed a new ID badly. Sorry, man."

"Why did you do it?"

"Long story. I'd done time and I needed to have a fresh ID to get a real job."

Great.

"Murder?" I ask.

"No way, never killed nobody."

"So what did you do time for?"

"Why go there, man? I don't wanna feel rotten. I'm a new man now—thanks to you. Look at it this way, I saved your life once, but you're saving my ass every day, buddy." Chen uses his second beer glass to clink mine on the table.

"I'm very grateful, really," I say, "but you're putting me in a precarious position, forcing me to share my name, my driver's license, my social, my credit report with you."

"Come on, man. Share the love, bro. Please don't tell the cops. If you tell the cops, I'll be stuck in there for life, man." Chen's talking at a hundred miles an hour, panicking.

"Just slow down, OK?" I say. "I didn't say I'd tell the cops. But what tells me you're not going to commit some other crime with my name on it?"

"Ah, come on, it's not like I'm gonna rob a bank, you know. I've been a stellar employee. You didn't see the paper?"

"Sure, I saw the paper. Why are you suddenly the good guy?" I say, dubious.

"I wanted to do something good for a change."

"Just like that?" I take a few sips of beer.

"You don't believe me?" he says.

The half-pounder the waitress brought remains untouched, its cheese solidifying, its fat congealing. I don't know what to do with this guy.

"How did you do it?" I say.

"What?" he asks.

"How did you change your life?"

"Well, the name helped. Got me a fresh start."

"I have the same name—it didn't exactly change *my* life," I say.

"Change is slow," says Chen. "At first, I just bluffed my way through—what else can I do? Then stuff started happening. I got the job. Got the apartment. Got the girl."

"At least someone got the girl." The beer is seeping through my insides now, a deep warmth I haven't felt in a long time.

"Nice girl too." Chen grins.

"You're happy in your new life?"

"Beats the lock up. I don't complicate my life like the rich folks out there. Crime got hard, you know. Time to move on, try some honest living. Shed the dead skin and slither away. You play poker?"

"Maybe, I don't really remember."

"See, I learned a few things about life from poker," he says. "Even when you're dealt a bad hand—like a measly two—you can still bluff your way to the jackpot. Or you might get lucky and end up winning with three twos, see. But if you wanna win, you can't fold early. Life's just like that." He finishes off his second glass of beer. "You've got a two of spades in your life? Or were you one of those guys born with a silver spoon up your ass?" The booze is loosening him up.

"Of course I have a two of spades." Without thinking, I pat the envelope in my pocket.

"What's in there anyway?" Chen flicks his chin toward the manila envelope that's sticking out of my vest pocket. "You had that with you in the alley too."

It's uncanny how much this guy knows about me.

"I lost my wife," I say.

"Hmm, sorry, man."

I can't believe I'm telling him this.

"I don't know how she died. She has no grave and no ashes. It can't be good."

"It's *never* good," he says, then finishes off his second glass. "So what's in there?"

He's pointing to the envelope. I don't feel like telling him.

"They're like her ashes," I say.

He looks horrified.

"You can't be carrying around a dead person's ashes like that, bringing them into a bar with the living. Dead people gotta be buried, man."

"Never mind. I'd like some hot tea when the waitress comes around," I say, feeling cold again.

"She ain't coming around anytime soon. Woman knows when to make herself scarce," says Chen. "And they don't got tea in here. You're not gonna drink that?" Chen points to the second untouched beer in front of me. "Don't know why I'm so thirsty."

I slide it over.

"Listen Chen, I'm not going to tell anyone. You saved my life. I'll lend you my name. It's a fair exchange—as long as you don't do anything to get us in trouble."

"Thanks, bro. I promise, I'll be straight and cool, and I won't abuse the situation." He shakes my hand. "And you don't be dying on me again. For one thing, those IRS guys can sniff out a dead man on payroll."

"All right, Chen, thanks for the beer."

54

Max

After the intense pow-wow with that strange Chen creature, I crave some fresh air. I flag a cab back to Santa Monica, and head to the beach.

On this cold, windy winter day, the ocean looks like the reservoir for all the tears humanity had ever shed. The marine layer blocks out the setting sun in a dense cloud. Kitchen lights glow from inside waterfront homes, as families sit down for dinner. I walk all the way to the end of the jetty and stare at the jagged, gray waves. My bones still feel chilled down to the marrow.

I retrieve the sealed manila envelope from my pocket. It's creased, stained, and the tape has peeled off.

It takes courage to open it, sure. But it also takes courage to never open it. Sylvia's words come back to me. Mourning Josephine almost destroyed me. Will reliving her last horrific days bring her back? What about grieving her once again?

No. Nothing in this world will bring her back to me. Only my own death could bring us back together. Maybe. Even then, it's a matter of debate.

Am I ready to end it now, so that I can—just maybe—see Josephine again? Alas, I'm a romantic, but I'm no Romeo. Being half dead hasn't worked very well either. I've tried it long enough. The last remaining option is choosing to live the rest of my natural life out. I'm still 29, damn it.

I kiss the manila envelope.

"My sweet Josephine, forgive me for staying on this earth a little longer than you."

Before I change my mind, my hands release the envelope, and it falls in the water. The sea takes it in her bosom, for the sea takes everything it is given.

"*Au revoir, mon amour.*"

The ink is slowly becoming one with the seawater—the ink that chronicles the tears I had shed in my previous life. I remain there, watching it. Will this act of cowardice or bravery change me? Will I be able to shed the old Max and slither away? I don't know. One can only try something different.

It's getting too dark and cold now. My bandaged fingers are numb again. I walk away, four pages lighter. Then I head to Pascal's for a hot meal.

55

Max

At Quatre Epingles, I sit beside the fire pit in the courtyard to warm up. I order a Bordeaux and hot soup, and scrape the *L.A. Times* off a table, blocking out the happy-hour crowd. I turn to the sad headlines this time, the bread and butter of what we call news.

Soon, Pascal finds me. One of the waiters must have told him I'm here. The French chef gently pulls the newspaper aside to get a better look at me.

"I knew the food was bad in Antarctica. Look at you." He pinches my arm to gauge the damage. "*Allez*, dinner on the house after all that bloody snow. You can't be eating soup by yourself after all that. What kind of world is this, anyway?" He sees the hollowness in my eyes, and gives me a big slap on the back. "It must be a really bad day if you're not even rinsing your eyes in the beauty here tonight." Pascal tilts his head toward the back room.

I look past the salad-pecking, Perrier-guzzling canopy of

California blonds. Two brunettes bite into Croque Monsieurs and lick the melted gruyère off their lips. I immediately recognize the lips I had so longed to bite into again, the soothing exotic eyes that had kept me company in the vastness of the snow, in the constriction of my cell. I have worshipped this intangible goddess for as long as I can remember. Just then Dr. Rani looks up and sees me from across the room.

The moment she recognizes me, her mouth blossoms into a smile. When her eyes land on my bandaged fingers, they soften into concern. She waves at me to join their table.

I stare at her from afar, frozen. I don't want to admit it, but I thought of her every day since I had last seen her. It is she who has kept me alive this whole time. All of her encapsulated essence comes back to me now: the two dots of bergamot perfume on her warm nape; her fluttery touch; her easy laughter; her serious voice telling me to be nice to my body; her quick intellect; her comforting breasts; and her kisses, each speaking its own language of passion.

I realize then that as little as I know Rani, thanks to the amnesia, I actually know her more than any other woman in my life. Today, she is the only tangible reality. It is only her touch that I remember, only her voice, only her eager lips. That must be a gift from the universe. An ace of hearts.

Rani beckons to me again. Could she have missed me? Her eyes are so open tonight that in them, I can see my future.

"Come on, be a man," goads Pascal.

I ignore him, and set the newspaper down with its long bill of unread tragedies. Then I walk to Rani's table, praying for a miracle.

ABOUT THE AUTHOR

Nel Stephenson is a New Yorker transplanted to Los Angeles. He's a hybrid, at home in the snooty ivory tower, and riding the late night "L" in Chicago. He was raised by feisty women with a sense of humor, and was taught to swear like an Italian. When he's not writing, he's surfing in the shark-infested waters of SoCal. Drop him a line and tell him what you love and what you hate.

NelStephenson.com

NelStephenson@outlook.com

ACKNOWLEDGMENTS

Many thanks to Ray for endless conversations about the book; to Ed, Antarctica Mike, Skye Moody, and Blythe for their generous consultations; and all the patient early readers who helped pare down all the fat. My hat to Matt Addis for finding his inner Chen—and taking us on a great audiobook ride.

Made in the USA
San Bernardino, CA
24 May 2020

72292135R00146